MW01229182

Kayah's Tears

Leigh Titler

Fantaisiocht Publishing, Mississippi

ASIN: B0BCX8DLSK
ISBN: 9798392332236

First paperback addition April 2023

Cover design by: Twisted Wolf Graphix
Edited by Gloria Titler, Jill Smith

Published by Fantaisiocht Publishing, Mississippi

Printed in the United States of America

This book is dedicated to Spring Olson. I found the other half of my soul when I married my husband. God only knew I gained something else that would change my life forever. We ran around the same group of friends our whole lives but never found each other. We first met each other through a job in passing. But then you came back into my life when I needed it the most. I was broken and only the shell of my former self. Spring, you were the sunshine in the rain that made the storm bearable. Little by little, you encouraged me to pick up my broken soul and put it back together after I was hurt. All my life, the wolf has been my spirit animal. I have always found strength in these beautiful animals. That is why you are my Kayah. You helped me find the strength I needed to heal, and you were able to help me hear what everyone else had been telling me all along. Thank you! I love you, and I am proud to call you my sister.

Contents

Part One:

The Nightmare

"The thing about nightmares was that you couldn't prepare for them. They sneaked up on you when you were most vulnerable."
— Sylvia Day.

Chapter 1

The sound of her paws pounding the ground was all Kayah could hear as she ran into the swampy woods just outside New Orleans in the dead of night. Running is the only way to keep her past from plaguing her future. Even as a small child Kayah had been cursed with the memories from that dreadful night when her parents were killed, and she was branded an orphan. The difference between now and then she could run for hours in the moonlight instead of hiding in her closet crying until the morning light.

Growing up was not easy for Kayah. She may have grown up in the home of the Alpha of the Dire wolves, but most of the pack did not see her as a member. Kayah only spoke to a few wolves in the pack, but the rest kept her at more than arm's length. Kayah is a beautiful Timber wolf with gray and white fur, ice-white eyes, and an electric blue ring close to the pupil. As a human, she is five foot and nine inches tall, has shoulder-length brown hair, blue eyes, and a curvy body.

Forty-five minutes earlier...

Kayah sat on her bed with her knees drawn up, where she rested her head. Beads of sweat slid down her spine and pooled at the base of her back. Her sweating had nothing to do with it being a summer night in July and ninety-eight degrees. The nightmares have returned, causing her to relive the night that changed her life forever.

The Nightmare........

On Christmas eve night, Kayah was kneeling on a chair, helping her mom place cookies on a plate for Santa's biggest night of the year. Asheara looked down at her giggling child, feeling that her life was complete.

"Can I carry the plate, mommy?" asked a wide-eyed Kayah.

"Why don't you let mommy help? That way, Santas' cookies won't slide off the plate," said Asheara.

"Otay, Mommy," Kayah said while rubbing her sleepy eyes.

After taking the plate off the counter, she held her other hand for Kayah to take. Together they walked into the living room and up to the tall barstool next to the Christmas tree.

"Turn them on, mommy!"

"Turn what on, Kayah?"

"The Wites! How will Santa find us if the Tristmas tree wites are off?"

Giving a little chuckle, Asheara sat down the plate of cookies and bent to plug in the lights when she heard the back door slam.

"Nyko, is that you?" asked Asheara.

"Yes, Asheara, and where is my princess?"

Running up to Nyko and lifting her arms, "Here I am, papa... Up!"

Nyko lifted Kayah in the air and turned in a circle, making

her laugh. He lowered her down just a little bit and wrapped his arms around her, snuggling into her neck, tickling her with the stubble on his unshaven face making her giggle.

"Oh, my sweet little princess, I have missed you today. But now it is time for you to go to bed so Santa can come and visit. We will have plenty of time to play tomorrow."

"But I not tired, papa," said a very sleepy Kayah as he used the palms of her hands to rub her eyes.

"Hold her a minute and sway. You will put her right to sleep," said Asheara.

Looking down at his wife and lifetime mate, he smiled and started to sway. It wasn't long before Kayah laid her head on Nyko's shoulder.

As Kayah slowly drifted to sleep in her papa's arms, she heard the murmurings of her parent's conversation.

"Nyko, what is wrong? I could see the worry in your eyes when you came home," asked Asheara.

"I spotted hunters as I was leaving the clubhouse...."

"Hunters, what were they doing in our area?" Asheara asked.

"I think they are still upset that we would not patch over into their club. I refused to let them run guns in my territory. I refuse to let our daughter or the other pups grow up in a rogue MC club. Plus, we will not mix our packs. Timberwolves do not mix with gray wolves," Nyko said.

"I have a terrible feeling you have started a war, Nyko. What are you going to do then if they come and bring violence to our pack and club? What are you going to do then?"

"Quiet women!" Nyko barked. "I am your Alpha and the president of this club. I may let you get away with many things because you are my old lady. I am telling you now; you will remember your place in this club and this pack. You are a Beta, and my old lady, that is it."

"You have forgotten one thing, Nyko. I am also the mother of your pup. Now I will tell you, you will not talk to me like I am just another bitch in the pack or just a biker groupie that is hoping to be made an old lady someday. Plus, I will stand up to you when I think you are doing something that can put our pup in danger. The Hunters are ruthless. They are the type of wolves that would kidnap Kayah, and when she comes into her first heat, they will force a pair bond on her. She is the first Omega born in an Alpha line in years. She is the first female pup that could be Alpha one day, or did you forget that?" she asked.

Nyko kissed Kayah on her head before he laid her down on the couch. He turned to face his mate, and his anger melted away; he knew she was right. He kissed her gently and softly rubbed her arms, "I will give Colby a call and let him know what is going on and see what he has to say."

"Good! I am going to put our daughter to bed, and we can finish talking while you eat dinner," Asheara said.

Asheara overheard the last part of Nyko's phone conversation when she stepped into the kitchen. After he hung up, she asked, "Why were you talking about Kayah to Colby?"

"It is called being proactive and protecting my family."

"So what did he say?"

"He is coming over tonight, and we are going to come up with a plan to take to the next club meetings. Plus, I have set in motion if anything ever happens to me, you and Kayah will be looked after."

"Nyko, I do not need to be looked after. Nothing will happen because you are going to figure this out."

"The future is not guaranteed, Asheara. As your Alpha and club president, that is my ruling you will obey."

Asheara knew it was not a good idea to push him, "As you wish, Nyko."

Without saying another word, she went to work warming Nyko his plate of food. After he was done eating, they sat on the couch, talking about their day and the joy she had in making cookies with Kayah.

"You know, Nyko, Kayah will be four at the end of August," she said while smiling.

"Hmm, I think that means it is time to give Kayah a brother

or sister," Nyko said with a twinkle.

"Oh really, you think so?"

Just as Nyko's lips covered Asheara's, he heard the rumble of motorcycles.

He pulled back smiling and said, "Well, I guess it is business first," then he gave her a quick peck on the cheek.

"I am going to check on Kayah," she said with a laugh.

Nyko nodded, then went to the door.

As Asheara bent to kiss her child's forehead, she heard a ruckus followed by a thud coming from the living room. She closed the door quietly and went to see what all the noise was about. When she turned the corner, the sight that she saw caused her to scream. She found Nyko bloody and lying motionless on the floor with a tall, bald-headed man with a black beard, holding a bloody pipe in his hand. Before she could run, two other men grabbed ahold of her.

The man with the pipe gripped Asheara's chin with a strong grip and said, "Where is that pretty little pup of yours?"

"Go to hell," she spat.

Without a blink of an eye, the man let go of her chin, smiled, and backhanded her, splitting her lip and bruising her cheek. He gripped her chin and turned her head so he could look into her eyes, and asked again, "Where is Kayah?"

"She's not here. You will never get your hands on her," she said, hoping that Kayah was in her secret hiding spot.

"Why must you make this difficult? Just tell me where I can find that pretty little pup of yours, and all this will be over," said the man.

Asheara turned her head, ripping her chin out of the man's grip, refusing to look at him. The man laughed and told one of the other men to get a chair and tie Nyko up. Once Nyko was bound to the chair, they slapped him in the face a couple of times to bring him around.

The screams from her mother were what woke Kayah. She crept to her bedroom door and noticed strange men in her house. Kayah snuck out of her room and over to the unique door her dad had made; he told her to hide in there if anything wrong happened. The only bad thing about her hiding spot was that she could see everything happening to her parents.

She watched as they tied up her dad and mom and held a gun to her mother's head.

"Where is the pup?" the bearded one asked Nyko.

"You will never find her," Nyko said, then spit at one of the intruders.

"So I take it we are going to do this the difficult way," the bearded one laughed. Then he looked at the other two and said, "Strip the bitch!"

Kayah watched in horror as they ripped off her mother's clothes. Kayah watched as each one of these intruders took their turn in raping her mother. They had her bound to where Asheara could not shift into her wolf form and fight back; all she could do was weep. When they were done rapping her, they turned back to the questions.

"I will ask again, where is Kayah?"

When Nyko would not answer, he nodded, and the one with long brown hair pulled back in a low ponytail pulled out a knife and dragged the blade across different parts of her mother's naked body. With every cut, Nyko cried out for his mate. It wasn't long before Asheara was covered in blood. When her parents would not tell them where she was, one of the men lifted a gun, and she watched as they put a bullet in her mother's skull.

Kayah covered her mouth, trying not to cry out, when she saw her strong Alpha father weeping over the loss of his mate. Then she watched as the bearded man who asked the question put the gun to her father's head and pulled the trigger. Then he barked orders at the other two men.

"The pup must be here. Sniff her out."

Two other men were told to search the house for Kayah while the bearded man placed her parents' bodies on the couch and cut the patches off her father's leather. When one of the men walked past her hiding spot, she got a good look at the patches on the leather vests. One said Vice President, and the patch said, Hunters. She had heard her father talk about them when she was falling asleep. Knowing these were the bad men her father was talking about, she knew she needed to be very quiet.

After they decided that Kayah was not in the house, the intruders left. Kayah came out of her hiding spot and went to her parents. When Kayah screamed, it forced her to shift for the first time. Her joints popped, and bones shifted under her skin. Her nose became a muzzle, her hands and feet became paws, and she grew a tail. Kayah's skin transformed to gray and white fur. When her transformation was complete, she jumped up on the couch and lay across her parent's laps.

What seemed to be hours later, there was a knock at the door; Kayah let out a low growl in fear the intruders had returned. When Colby opened the door, he knew he was too late. Kayah just howled while she lay across the laps of her parents. When Colby's Sargent of arms tried to move Kayah, she growled. When he reached to pick her up, she bit down on his arm, making him retreat.

"Let me try and talk to her," said Colby.

"Kayah, my name is Colby. Nyko, your father, was a good friend of mine. He asked me to come over tonight and help him. I am so sorry, Kayah, I was too late. He asked me to care for you if anything ever happened to him."

Kayah laid her head down and whimpered; when he reached out. When she was quiet, he carefully picked Kayah up and cradled her in his arms. Colby looked at his Sargent of Arms and said, "Sid, call someone to help you clean this up. I also need you to get someone out here and get some things for Kayah. Make sure you clean up her father's leather."

"What will you do with the pup and the leather?" Sid asked.

"I am taking Kayah home with me. I will save her father's leather and give it to her when she is old enough to understand it."

"Colby, man, she is a Timberwolf; the pack will shun her.

They will never see her as part of the pack," Sid warned.

"Did I ask you your concerns? Kayah is a unique wolf, and she needs to be protected. The only way I know she will be protected is with me. Now, as your Alpha, obey!"

"What makes her so special?"

"She is an Omega from an Alpha bloodline," Colby said, looking down at Kayah.

"You are telling me she is from the Ancient bloodline?"

"Yes, there are only a few who know. I trust you to keep your mouth shut and help me protect this child."

Sid pulled out his phone without saying another word and made the arrangements. It wasn't long before the house was crawling with the Bayou Wolves. Colby sat on the porch swing and waited for his old lady to show up so she could take Kayah home. When he finally saw the headlights, he sighed with relief; Chloe was much better with children. Chloe slammed the truck door and ran to where Colby was sitting.

"Oh, the poor baby! Is this Kayah?" she asked.

"Yes, from the looks of her, she saw everything. She is going to need a bath. Her fur is matted with blood. When I walked in, she was lying on her parent's lap. She bit Sid, and he knows her secret."

"Why did you tell Sid? Colby, the more people know about her, the more danger she is in."

"Chloe, don't you think I know that?" he said quietly.

"She has finally fallen asleep? How is she able to shift so soon?" she asked.

"I think so... I also think the trauma she witnessed tonight is what forced her to shift at such a young age. It was the Hunters, and only Kayah can tell us who they were."

"Chloe, take her home and bathe her. See if you can talk her into shifting back."

"I will try. Come here, baby girl," Chloe said while picking her up.

Kayah let out a whimper as she settled into Chloe's arms. Chloe placed Kayah in the truck's front seat and climbed behind the wheel. She looked up at Colby and knew he was hurting from the death of his friend. She watched as he joined the others inside the house. When the door shut, she backed down the driveway and drove home.

Seventeen years later....

Kayah knew someone was following her; she was not in the mood for company, so she pushed harder. The faster she ran, the better she felt. But her tagalong was still close behind her. She quickly turned left to head deeper into the woods when she felt her follower was no longer behind her. Kayah decided it was time to start running back into safer territory now that she had lost her follower. Just as she was about to jump a fallen tree, she was met with bright yellow eyes. Kayah slid to a stop and stared at the pure black wolf that blocked her path. The black wolf jumped off the tree and stood in front of Kayah. To avoid the conflict that was about to start, Kayah leaped over the wolf and kept running. Kayah was bigger than the wolves in her pack because she was the only Timberwolf in a Dire wolf pack.

When Kayah returned home, she saw her tagalong sitting on her front porch; she shifted and headed for her front door.

"Go home, Demon. I didn't want to talk to you in the woods, and I don't want to talk now," she snapped.

"Come on, Kayah; you have been dodging my calls all week. Talk to me, please; the pack is starting to talk because you have quit attending the pack meetings," he pleaded.

"Demon, you know that the pack doesn't accept me. The only reason they tolerated me was that your parents raised me after my parents were killed. They know it is coming up on my twenty-first birthday, and it will be time for me to mate. So like I said, there is nothing to talk about. Now go away."

"Kayah, there is a mate out there for you. I think…"

"Demon, stop. I am a Timberwolf in a Dire wolf pack. There is no future for me."

"I know there is a Dire wolf that likes you."

"Who is it, Demon? Bear, Lucas… no, let me guess, it is Marc.

I don't have time for this. I need to take a shower and get ready for work. Just go away and leave me alone."

"It is me, Kayah. I am the one who likes you. I would be lucky to have you as a mate."

Kayah laughed so hard she gripped her stomach, "Demon, you know that will never work. You are in line to be Alpha. They would never let the Dire wolf Alpha mate with a Timberwolf orphan."

Kayah had officially pissed him off. Demon walked over to Kayah and grabbed her shoulders, and shook her. "Kayah, I don't give a fuck that you are a Timberwolf. You are intelligent, strong, brave, and beautiful. I don't care where you came from; I only care who you are now. Plus, who cares what the pack thinks? I will be the Alpha of this pack, and what I say goes."

Before he released her, Demon kissed her, making her see stars. "Now, no more running away from me. Do you understand?"

Kayah tipped her head and looked at Demon; without saying

a word, she went into her house and shut the door.

∞∞∞

He watched the exchange between the two young wolves and didn't like what he saw. But he knew that he went undetected like always. He had been watching Kayah since the night her parents were killed. Then, as he ran, he remembered the night a young Omega howl pierced his thoughts. It was like he had no control over his actions. When it happened, he was in the middle of a hunt; he lost the scent of his prey and started running to the howl stuck in his head. He ran on autopilot to the house, crawling with bikers. He watched a man holding a tiny pup in his arms, rocking in the porch swing, trying to calm the pup covered in blood. That is when he realized that he was undetectable by other wolves, so he watched from the shadows. He watched as headlights came down the road and turned into the driveway. A small petite woman jumped out of the truck, slammed the door, and ran up to the pup and the man. They talked briefly, then she took the pup and returned to the truck. When the truck backed down the driveway and pulled away, he stayed in the shadows and followed the truck to the swamps of New Orleans.

Chapter 2

Kayah went straight to the shower and stripped; she stood under the hot water going over their conversation. She didn't know how it had turned to where Demon had the upper hand. All she could think about was the kiss. Kayah could still feel Demon's lips on her, and they still tingled from where they touched. She had always thought he looked at her like a sister. There is no way that Colby or the pack will ever let her and Demon become mates. She would always carry the title of an outcast, and she had come to terms with the fact that she would always be alone.

When the water had finally run cold, she shut the water off, stepped out of the shower, and dried off. She needed to get Demon out of her head before she went to work. Kayah stood before the fogged-over mirror and focused her thoughts as she wiped the condensation from the mirror. *I can not think about him. It will never happen. You will get control again. I was able to avoid him for the past few weeks; I can do it again.* Kayah closed her eyes and took a deep breath. When she breathed out, her mind was clear and focused once more.

As Kayah finished her makeup, she heard her front door slam, and a voice that would always make her smile rang out.

"Hey, heifer, are you ready? She-bitch, where are you?" yelled Dezra.

"I am back here. How many times have I told you not to call me She-bitch. I am not a werewolf. I am a Timberwolf," Kayah yelled back.

"Well, you are my She-bitch, and there is nothing you can do about it," Dezra said, leaning on the door jam.

"Oh, come on, I am not fittin' to fight with you today. We are going to be late," Kayah said, looking at her watch and pushing past her.

Dezra has been Kayah's best friend since Colby introduced

Kayah to the pack. Dezra has always been a vision and was promised to be mated with Shilo. She was five foot five inches tall and had the darkest chocolate-brown skin and deep brown eyes. In her wolf form, she was a pure white wolf with dark brown eyes. Out of all the pack members, she knew Dezra would always have her back. She was that kind of friend, her ride or die.

As Dezra climbed into Kayah's pink jeep, she said, "On the way home, we need to stop at the store."

"What the hell do you need now? We just went to the store a couple of days ago," Kayah asked.

"I need more cacoochie sausage; I ran out this morning."

"Dezra, it is called Conecuh. Con neck kah. How can you eat it and not know what it is called?"

"Bitch, who asked you?" Dezra laughed.

"I'm just saying, you need to know what it is called," Kayah laughed.

"Oh, and when will you make that soup again?" Dezra asked

with a smile.

"What are you wanting now, Dezra? What soup?"

"Zuppa Da Coochie!" she said, smirking.

"Oh, my life... Dezra, it's called Zuppa Toscanna. You need to say things correctly; what happens if I am not around and you need to ask someone? They are going to look at you like you have lost your damn mind," Kayah said, shaking her head.

Dezra knew how to say the name right... she wanted to make her friend smile. She had seen that her dear friend had another rough night, and it still had its evil claws in her now. Dezra could not handle seeing that haunted look in Kayah's eyes whenever she talked about the nightmares that made her run all night, so she would find ways to make her smile. The silence in the jeep was becoming uncomfortable, and she could see that Kayah was still struggling to pull herself together. So, she turned on the radio and turned up the volume to ear-piercing.

Then they jammed to music for the rest of the ride to work,

leaving the night that hunted Kayah unsaid.

∞∞∞

Kayah worked through her day on auto-pilot. With her being a Surg Tech, the day seemed to drag out with no surgeries scheduled. Kayah sat at the nurse's station working on patients' charts when Dezra scared the shit out of her.

"Girl, forty-five minutes left, and we get to ditch this bitch for the day."

"Dammit, Dezra! Why must you always do that?" asked a frustrated Kayah.

"Kayah, you are a fuckin wolf. How do you not pay attention to your surroundings? One day that shit will get you killed, then I would lose my mind and go bat shit crazy," Dezra said while leaning a hip on the desk.

"Fuck off, Dezra. I am not in the mood for your bullshit today," Kayah snapped.

"Whoa... whoa... whoa... Slow your roll She-Bitch; there is

no need for your attitude."

"I'm sorry. I want this day over with. It has been slow, and I am feeling off," she apologized.

Dezra studied Kayah's face and could still see that the nightmare that had haunted her the night before lingered just below the surface. "We are down to five minutes. Let's get the hell out of here."

Kayah smiled and nodded while closing the chart she had just finished. Kayah felt like a ticking time bomb from all the pent-up unspent energy that she held. When she was safely out of the hospital parking lot, Kayah punched down on the gas making Dezra grab the chicken stick and cuss at her. Kayah laughed all the way to Walmart. After they each grabbed what they needed from the store, they climbed back into her jeep and drove home.

When Kayah pulled into her driveway, the annoyance she had battled all day had returned. Demon was sitting on her porch with his hands clasped behind his head and feet kicked out, making himself at home.

"Girl, what is Demon doing here?" Dezra asked.

"To be a pain in my ass."

"Do you want me to stay?"

"No, go home. It will be okay."

"Am I picking you up for work tomorrow?" asked Dezra.

"No, You are all on your own. I started my vacation today."

"Oh yeah, that's right. You took a month off work. Why did you take that much time off again?"

"Because I need some time to myself. It is coming up on my twenty-first birthday. So I want some freedom to run," Kayah said quietly.

"You know I am here for you if you need me."

"I know. That's why I love you. Now go home."

"Okay, but call me later and tell me why Demon is sitting on your porch as if he has moved in. Has he moved in?"

"Girrrl...Boo... Go home, Dezra."

"Fine! I will talk to you later."

When Dezra was gone, she climbed the steps to her porch and kicked Demon's feet. "Go Home!"

"Well, that was a rude greeting," he said.

"No one asked you to be here. So go away, Demon."

"Now you keep being mean; I will take you over my knee and teach you some manners," he threatened.

"Demon, I am getting tired of telling you to go away. Now buzz off. I don't want to visit anyone. So, I will heat some leftovers and get drunk on my Crown Apple."

"How did you get the liquor? You are not twenty-one yet," asked Demon with a raised eyebrow.

Scowling, Kayah replied, "How many times do I need to tell you? You're not my mate, and you're not my Alpha. Go away."

"Okay, okay, I will stop harping on you. Please let me cook you a good steak, and we can drink a nice bottle of wine," he pleaded.

Kayah gave Demon a funny look and said, "You are not that slick."

"Kayah, I am just trying to be your friend. I know this time of year is hard for you. So please just let me be your friend."

Kayah studied Demon's face and decided he was telling the truth, "A steak does sound good."

"See... Let me cook for you, and you can sit back with your feet up."

"If I let you cook for me, will you leave me alone?" she asked.

"Let's get through dinner first," Demon said, smiling.

Kayah finally relented and let Demon in so he could cook. She sat at her kitchen table, drinking a glass of red wine, and watched Demon move around her kitchen as if he cooked there every day. He stood at her counter with a towel tossed over his shoulder and chopped onions and mushrooms to saute that would top the steak. When the butter hit the hot cast-iron pan, she sniffed the air. She could smell the garlic he used to rub the steaks when he placed them in the buttered pan. She moaned when she caught the scent of the sizzling steak.

"How do you know how to cook?" she asked.

"I learned from my uncle," he said without turning around.

Kayah gawked at the plate Demon sat in front of her. The steak was perfectly cooked with a pile of mushrooms and onions. He also cooked fried potatoes and brussels sprouts. Kayah and Demon talked like they used to when they were kids like no time had passed while they ate. After eating, he insisted on cleaning up the mess from dinner so she could relax. Demon could also see what made her run night after night, still clung to her. After dinner, they decided to watch a movie. Kayah studied Demon, and she would never admit it, but she enjoyed spending time with Demon and seeing him in her space. It was the first in a very long time she felt free, and she spent the night watching Madea movies and laughing until her belly hurt. She studied him when she knew that Demon was engrossed in the movie.

She had always thought he was the sexiest black man she had ever laid her eyes on, which made it hard to grow up in the house she was raised in. But, now that he was an adult, he was mouth-watering, drop-dead sexy. Demon was over six foot and had the prettiest dark chocolate brown skin. He kept his head shaved bald and had a goatee. She had trouble not getting lost in his eyes when she looked at him; they were dark brown with a light yellow ring close to the pupil. But she knew that it would never work. He came from a line of Dire Wolf alphas, and she was the outcast. So to save her heart and avoid the problems ahead, she decided to keep him only as a friend. Somehow she would need to get that through Demon's thick head.

When she had fallen asleep, he stayed close in case the nightmare returned. Then, almost precisely at midnight, Kayah started to whimper, and he knew the nightmare had returned. Demon wanted to hold her and chase the nightmare away, but he knew she would fight him.

"Kayah, wake up. It is just a dream," Demon said softly.

Kayah jumped like she had been stuck with a hot poker, and her eyes were wild, almost feral. Without saying a word, she ran for the front door. Again, she needed to run, but this time Demon would not allow her to run alone. By the time Demon had reached the front door, he had found scattered pieces of clothing. He spotted Kayah on the edge of her property at the tree line waiting for him. Demon quickly shed his clothing and shifted. When Demon was close enough, Kayah took off into the woods, knowing he was close behind. They ran for hours, and when the sun was about to rise, Kayah turned and headed back toward her house. When Demon was at the edge of the woods, he saw her naked ass as she turned the corner of her home and disappeared.

When he entered the house, he could hear the shower running, so he went to the kitchen, cleaned himself up, and waited on the couch for her to emerge from the bathroom. Demon relaxed some when he heard the water turn off. When Kayah came out of the bathroom, she was wrapped in a towel and said, "Thank you for the run. If you leave, please lock the door behind you. If you are going to stay, you can catch some sleep on the couch." Then she turned down the hallway. He smiled when he heard her shut and lock the bedroom door.

Demon woke to the smell of coffee brewing and Kayah cooking breakfast. She knew he watched her, "You are welcome to some coffee; food will be ready shortly," Kayah said without turning around.

After pouring himself a cup of coffee, he sat at the table and asked, "So, what are your plans today?"

"My vacation starts today. But, first, I need to head to Lowes and pick up the supplies to fix some things on this house."

"Are you going to go into bitch mode if I offer to hang out and help?"

"Demon, what are you doing?" she asked, setting down his plate.

"I am offering my friend help. Because I have a huge truck, and she has a little ass Jeep," he smiled while scooping up some eggs.

Shaking her head, "Demon, you irritate my soul. Now shut the fuck up and eat your breakfast."

Kayah and Demon spent the morning together looking at paint samples and picking up the stuff she needed to work on her house. When they pulled into her driveway, she rolled her eyes and said, "Fuck. This is going to be fun."

"What?" he asked.

"Your father is sitting on my porch," Kayah said as he jumped out of the truck slamming the door.

"Hello, Colby; what brings you to my door?" Kayah asked.

"Good afternoon, Kayah. I came out here concerned, but I see Demon is looking after you."

"Kayah does not need someone to look after her. She is capable of taking care of herself."

"Thank you, Demon. I can also answer for myself. Now, why are you here, Colby?"

"As I said, I wanted to check on you. You have missed the last five pack meetings, and I wanted to see if you were still alive."

"I am not going to any more pack meetings, Colby. The pack has never accepted me. They have made it clear I never have been and will never be a part of this pack. Now, if you excuse me, I have work to do," said Kayah as she turned her back to him.

"Kayah!" Colby barked. "You may not see this pack as your own, or me as your Alpha. I am an Alpha, and you will show me with respect."

Anger filled Kayah, and her eyes glowed when she turned to stand her ground. "Back off, Colby. My father was an Alpha. His blood runs through my veins, or did you forget that? You will show me some respect by remembering I am not just a Bitch in your pack. Now I said back off."

"Come on; you two knock it off. Kayah has a point. You are not her Alpha, and the pack does not see her as a member—only a few members accept her as part of the pack," Demon said, trying to defuse the ticking time bomb.

The furry died in Colby's eyes when he remembered the little pup he rescued all those years ago.

"Kayah, you are a member of this pack. Chloe and I raised you. I have something for you; come by the house for dinner. I think it is time we talked," Colby said.

Kayah studied the man that rescued and raised her. He had dark chocolate skin and eyes, just like Demon. Demon inherited a lot of traits from Colby. The only difference is that Colby had a broader chest and stood almost three inches taller than Demon.

Shaking her head, she asked, "What is so important?"

"Please, Kayah, come to dinner. Chloe misses you, and we can talk more," pleaded Colby.

Kayah let her anger fade and looked at the man who raised her. Then she remembered the kindness that could always be found in Chloe's soft brown eyes. She was a petite woman and a small wolf. Chloe had warm mocha brown skin and stood about five foot three. Chloe has always treated her like

a daughter, not some orphaned kid that they raised on a promise.

Relenting, she asked, "What time?"

"Come by about six."

"Okay, I will see you then. Now, excuse me; I have work I need to do."

Saying nothing, Colby stuck his hand in the front pocket of his jeans and nodded. He knew part of her problem with the pack was his fault; Colby had kept Kayah at arm's length when it came to the pack and the club. The more involved with the pack she got, the harder it would have been to keep her safe.

Colby walked back to his bike and climbed on. He watched his son help Kayah get supplies from his truck and carry them to the porch. Colby could see the Alpha in her by the way she carried herself. She was almost twenty-one and needed to know; on her birthday, she would ascend. Nothing was more painful than an Alpha wolf being branded a lone wolf and mateless. Somehow he needed to bring her back to the pack, she may be mateless, but she would have the pack as family. He noticed how his son looked at Kayah. If they ever became mates, her bloodline would take over his pack. That is one thing he would never let happen.

When Kayah heard the rumble of Colby's bike fade, she let out the breath she was holding.

She looked at Demon and could tell he wanted to say something. But, unfortunately, she was not in the mood.

"No, Demon, I don't want to talk about it. I want to work on my house and forget my shitty life."

"Okay, what are we going to work on first?"

"I want a deck. Let's tear out the porch and build a wrap-around deck."

"Rock on! I get to tear shit up too. This is the best day of my life," smiled Demon.

After they moved everything off the porch, they started the demo. Even with all the noise, her voice was loud and clear.

"Demon, will you go with me tonight?"

"Yes, Kayah, all you had to do was ask."

"Thank you," she said before prying up the next board.

Chapter 3

Kayah sat in Demon's truck staring at the house she was raised in, dreading what was to come. Demon could tell she was fighting with her emotions as he watched her through the windshield. Finally, Kayah opened the passenger door to the 4x4; she took a long breath and stepped out. She locked eyes with Demon and slammed the door, "I don't want to do this. I love your family but hate talking about that dreaded night."

"Kayah, we can leave; just get back in the truck, drive away now, and never look back."

"No, I made a promise to Colby. I don't back down from a commitment. I owe it to him to listen to what he needs to say. He took me in and raised me. He could have left me in the puddle of my parent's blood where he found me. Plus, your mom knows we are here; she is watching us through the kitchen window. Come on, let's get this night over," she said before walking to the house.

As Kayah raised her hand to knock, the door opened, and Chloe greeted them, "Kayah, you know you don't need to knock; this is your home. Hello, son. It is nice to see that you know where your house is," Chloe said as she hugged Kayah.

"Hi, mom," Demon said with a sheepish grin.

When Chloe finally let go, she smiled at Kayah, stepping aside and allowing them to enter the house. As Kayah made her way to the living room, she was flooded with memories from her childhood. She smiled at the memory of Demon chasing her and Dezra through the house and Colby yelling, 'Take it outside. This is a house, not the woods. A house is meant for living in, not running through."

Kayah was pulled from her thoughts when Demon placed a hand on her back, "Kai, are you okay?" he asked.

"Yeah, I am. I remember when Colby yelled at us when you chased Dezra and me through the house." she chuckled.

"Good times. You two were so mean to me. All I wanted to do was play with you, too," he said, sticking out his bottom lip.

"We were not mean to you. You always wanted to hang out with us. Did you ever think we just wanted some girl time?"

"Umm… No," he said with a puzzled expression.

"Well, we did. What girls want a stinky boy around all the time?"

"See, now you are just being mean again," he pouted.

She laughed, "Come on, let's go eat."

When they entered the dining room, Colby was already sitting at the head of the table. However, when Colby made eye contact with Kayah, he stood, showing her respect.

"Kayah, Son," he said with a nod. "Please be seated. Dinner will be served soon."

She sat in the same seat she had growing up, across from Colby.

"I need to tell you some things that might be unpleasant, but they are things you need to know. But first…," Colby said.

"Colby, for fuck sake, the girl just got here. This is the first time she has stepped into this house since her eighteenth birthday. Can we please at least eat in peace?" Chloe said as she slammed the platter of T-Bone steaks on the table.

"Like I was saying. First, I wanted to tell you how nice it is to have you home, even if it is just for a meal," said Colby as he sat back down.

The knot in Kayah's stomach loosened when she realized that they were going to eat first. Then, just like when she was a child, they waited until everyone was seated before the platters were passed around the big oak table. When the first bite of steak hit her tongue, she moaned, making Kayah and Demon smile. As she finished her twice-baked potato, Chloe sat down with a pear and mango cobbler.

"If your taste has not changed much, I know you loved my homemade cobblers," Chloe smiled.

Kayah smiled and said, "It looks delicious."

When dinner was over, they retired to the living room to

talk.

∞∞∞

"Babe, get us some beers, and get the box," Colby commanded.

Without a word, Chloe nodded and left the room. The room fell quiet, waiting for her return. Chloe returned with a box and three beers. After she gave out the beers, she gave her mate the small box and sat down.

"Kayah, how much do you remember from that night?" asked Colby.

"Everything," she said quietly.

Colby had always wondered if she remembered or if her brain had blocked out the memories, then decided to return in nightmares. No one knew what had happened except for Kayah. When they tried to talk to her about it when she was younger, she would shrug her shoulders.

"What do you mean everything, Kayah?" Colby asked.

"I remember my mother screaming, how they ripped her clothes off, tortured and raped then shot her. Then they executed my father after making him watch everything that was done to my mother. All because they were protecting me. Those BASTARDS killed my parents because of me. Is that good enough for you? Or do you want all the gory details?" Kayah said, panting.

"Kayah, that is not what I meant. I want to help you get justice for your parents and help you be at peace knowing the men who did this have paid for their sins. Remember, your father was like a brother to me. It kills me that my brother was taken from me, and it makes me furious that their pup had to grow up without them. You are the only one that can tell me who they were. Kayah, I need your help," Colby explained.

"Dad, why in the fuck would you bring this up now?" Demon asked.

"Because she is coming up on her twenty-first birthday and is a very special wolf. Kayah needs to know the truth," Colby said while standing.

Colby walked over to Kayah and held out the box for her to take. She stared at him, trying to decide if she wanted to know the secret the box held. Slowly she reached out, took the box from him, and sat it on her lap.

"What do you mean I am a special wolf?" she asked.

All Colby would say was, "Open the box, Kayah."

Kayah carefully gripped the folded flaps on the box and pulled them open. She froze at what she saw, causing angry tears to fall. She reached in and touched her father's leather. She looked up at Colby and asked, "Where are his patches?"

"They must have taken them when they left. I am sorry, Kayah, this is how we found it," Colby said sadly.

Kayah touched where the patches used to be and said softly, "I was very young when my parents were killed. But I remember the men that killed my parents were also wearing leather. I remember what their patches said because of being around my father's club members. The one I saw was tall with his hair pulled into a low ponytail, and the patches said Vice President, and the one below said, Hunters. He was the one that was told to search the house for me, but when I heard my mother scream, I ran to the hiding spot my father had made for me. I don't remember what the other two look like. Colby, why were they looking for me?" she asked.

"As I said, you are a special wolf."

"Colby, I am just a Timber Wolf. A normal Beta that had an Alpha for a father. There is nothing special about me."

"Kayah, it is my fault that the pack has kept you at arm's length. I have kept you from the pack because…you are the first Omega born in years. You are an Omega with Alpha blood in your veins," Colby explained.

"What the fuck does that mean?" she yelled.

"If someone forced a par bond with you for birthing pups, you would spawn an Alpha. They still hunt for you now," said Colby.

"I will kill anyone who comes for Kayah," spat Demon.

Colby noticed his son's reactions to what was being said and did not like it.

"So my parents were killed because they think I am an Omega. I remember the stories, Colby. You told us that Omegas come from an Ancient bloodline from a different world called Aadya. When Aadya was cursed, an Omega and her mate were said to escape to our world called Edan. That way, the five bloodlines would survive. After all these years, you're telling me you kept this a secret to protect me. I don't believe this, and I remember my father telling my mother that the Hunters were pissed off that he rejected them to patch into his club and pack. I think you are feeding me a line of bullshit. You say you want to help me, that you love me like one of your own, but yet you tell me that you have kept me separate from the pack. Plus, I would know if I were an Omega, I would be pure white as a wolf, and my eyes would be a brilliant blue. That would also make me a werewolf, not just a Timber Wolf. I am done with this conversation. Colby, you no longer need to worry about me. Your pack doesn't want me, and I don't need them. I became at peace awhile ago that I would never have a mate," said Kayah letting her anger grow.

Demon grabbed her hand and said, "Kayah, I told you, I want you as my mate. I don't care you are a Timber Wolf; I love you for who you are."

"No, Demon, you can not claim her as your mate. As your Alpha and your father, I forbid it. Now you will obey," barked Colby.

"See, even your father finds me unworthy, and he raised me. I forgot he raised me because he promised my father he would ensure I was cared for. Well, I am full-grown now. I don't need looking after," said Kayah, putting the box under her arm. Kayah looked at Demon and said, "Don't worry about giving me a ride home. I can take care of myself."

Kayah stormed out of the house, letting the door slam; she finally took a deep breath when Demon's voice could only be heard as a whisper.

∞∞∞

Demon was filled with rage; when he opened the door, he almost ripped it off its hinges. By the time Demon reached his father, his vision was tinged in red.

"Why the fuck would you treat her that way?" screamed Demon.

"I told her the truth, Demon. I have never lied," Colby said calmly.

"YOU!" he turned to his mother. "You say you love her like she was your pup, but yet you don't say anything to protect her from this dick," said Demon pointing at his father.

"Demon, sweetheart… Your father is the Alpha of this pack and the club president. Therefore, what he says is the law. I will not disobey your father and my Alpha. So you better smarten up, son, and fall in line," Chloe said quietly.

"NO, FUCK THAT! I love Kayah. She is the wolf I choose as my mate."

"Listen here, boy. I forbid you to mate with her. You have a responsibility to this pack. You will be Alpha one day. You will fall in line and obey, or there will be hell to pay. So now I will do what I said and help Kayah get justice for the death of her parents. But you will not claim her as yours; she is not of our kind," yelled Colby puffing up his chest.

Demon shook his head, then shoved his father back with both hands, "NO! Fuck that, fuck you, and fuck the pack. I will turn my back on all of you mother fuckers if it means I can be with Kayah. It does not bother me to be a lone wolf and step down from being Alpha." Then, with his mother crying after him, Demon walked out of the house he grew up in.

Chapter 4

Once again, he found himself watching from the shadows. His hyper-sensitive hearing allowed him to pick up on the conversation in the house. From the discussion, his suspicions were spot on. Kayah was an Omega that made her like him… well, almost like him. He agreed with the bastard Alpha about her mating with a Dire Wolf. Of course, that would never happen if he had anything to do with it. But he knew he needed to stay close to Kayah now. When she turned twenty-one, she would ascend to her full powers. When Kayah stormed out of the house, letting the door slam, his muscles bunched, making him shift positions breaking a stick. He froze when he saw that Kayah had also heard the stick break. She stopped, looked toward the sound, and saw a vast solid black mass with red and yellow orbs in the darkness. Afraid of being spotted, he closed his eyes and stayed very still. Kayah shook her head and continued walking down the driveway pulling her phone from her back pocket and calling the only person she knew had her back. Keeping a safe distance, he followed Kayah, never hearing what Demon said to his father.

∞∞∞

Dezra was sitting down to watch one of her favorite shows "A Christmas Story" when her phone rang.

"What's up?"

"I need you to come and pick me up."

"What the fuck for, Bitch? You got wheels."

"Dezra, come on, I need you right now. I am out by your Alpha's house and just had to deal with Colby and Demon's shenanigans. Please can you pick me up? I am walking down the damn road."

"What the fuck happened? I thought Demon's ass took you out there for dinner?"

"I will tell you when you get here. Just come and get me. I am tired of walking down this dark road."

"I will be right there."

Kayah sighed when she disconnected and shoved the phone into her back pocket. She would keep what she saw earlier to herself. It wasn't long before she saw the headlights of Dezra's car come down the road.

Dezra stuck her head out the car window and said, "Hurry up and get in the car. It is creepy as fuck out here."

After she placed the box in the backseat, Kayah climbed in the front, "Aww, a strong wolf like you is creeped out by some woods," she laughed.

"It's not the woods. It is what is in the woods. I thought I saw something."

"Then what are you waiting for? Let's get out of here."

Instead of turning around, Dezra zoomed past her childhood home. Kayah noticed that Demon's truck was no longer in the driveway, and Colby's bike was also gone. Silence filled the car, and Dezra watched Kayah out of the corner of her eye. She knew her friend was hurting and needed to talk, but she didn't know what to say. Finally, just as Dezra was going to turn on the music, Kayah spoke.

"He told me that I am an Omega."

"Really? I thought that was just a campfire story."

"That is all you have to say? Come on, Dezra, it is bullshit."

"You don't believe it?"

"No, for god's sake, if it was true, my parents were killed because of me. So I refuse to believe it. Plus, my parents would have told me. So that would also mean the other part of the story is true," said Kayah shaking her head.

"What other part?" Dezra asked.

"The part that the five bloodlines of wolves came from Aadya, and the four great queens of Aadya are the ones that saved the realms," she explained.

"Yeah, we came from somewhere, Kayah. So why do you find this hard to believe?" Dezra asked.

"Dezra, it is all crazy nonsense."

"Why? Because you have never seen it?"

"Well, yes. That means dragons, magic, Greek Gods, and much other crap is real. Magic is not real. Dragons are only found in storybooks, and Greek Gods are mythical," Kayah snorted in disgust.

"Kayah, you are just blind to everything around you. Think about it, we are wolves. Every time we shift into our wolf form, that is magic. When we par bond with our mate, the link that connects us for life is magic. So why is it so hard for you to believe that our ancestors came from a different world, realm, whatever your want to call it?"

Kayah folded her arms and sat back in the seat. She was quiet for a good five minutes.

"Okay, I will give you that, but what about the other things? For example, have you ever seen a dragon or a Greek God?" she asked.

"Kayah, you know I haven't. I think the world would know

if dragons were flying around and if the Greek Gods walked among us. So suck it up and deal with it."

"I can't. I just can't, Dezra... If I accept what Colby said, that means I am the reason my parents died."

"Kayah, your parents died because of some sick ass fuckers. Plus..."

Kayah cut Dezra off and said, "I remember everything from that night. It was another wolf pack and MC club that killed my parents. So I know who they are."

"How? Who told you?" she asked.

"No one told me. So I saw everything that happened and who did it."

"Why have you kept this quiet? Why did you never tell me?" Dezra asked, slamming the brakes and stopping in the middle of the road.

"That was the worst night of my life. I don't want to remember it, but it haunts me every night."

"Girl, you know you can count on me. You should've told

me."

"What the hell could you have done? Plus, I didn't want you to feel sorry for me like you do now."

"Sorry... I don't feel sorry for you. I am pissed for you. Some monsters broke into your house and killed your parents, and you watched. I feel sorry for the little girl you were and want justice for my best friend."

Kayah studied her closest friend and saw that she was telling the truth. She nodded and asked, "I hear you... I do. I will tell you about that night someday soon. But for now, can we please get moving before we get hit?"

Without saying anything, Dezra started driving again. As they drove past the clubhouse, she noticed Colby's bike was there, but Demon's truck was nowhere to be found.

"You know Colby also told me that me being an Omega is the reason he kept the pack at arm's length from me. Demon confessed his undying love for me, and Colby told me I am not good enough for the pack or his son because of my bloodline,"

Kayah said nonchalantly.

"Fuck that and fuck him. How could he say that he raised you? If he was going to keep you from the pack, why did he bring you to meetings? Demon loves you? I bet his dad loved that. What did you say?" asked Dezra.

"That he could go to hell. I don't need him or his pack," she said smugly.

"What the hell are you going to do about Demon?"

"Girl…I plan on avoiding him."

"Okay…so… your place or mine?" Dezra asked.

"Yours. Just go to your house, then you can drop me off in the morning before you go to work."

"Sounds good to me."

The rest of the drive was quiet. It was about ten p.m. when they arrived at Dezra's house; when Kayah entered the living room, she tossed the box and plopped down next to it on the couch.

"Girl… what is in that box? Please tell me you didn't bring

body parts in here."

"It ain't body parts, dumb ass. It's my father's leather; Colby gave it to me."

"Oh…what are you going to do with it?" asked Dezra.

"I don't know… I might try and find my father's pack…my pack," she said quietly.

Saying nothing else, Dezra tossed her a blanket, and she walked off, leaving Kayah to her thoughts.

∞∞∞

The nightmare returned like it did every night; she paced the living room, trying to calm the urge to run. Finally, when the need to run became more than she could handle, she quietly opened the front door, stepped onto the front porch, and froze. The red and yellow orbs were back. This time she was going to find out what they were. She stripped quickly and shifted. Kayah took off toward the glowing orb in the dark; when she was close enough, she noticed the spheres were a set of eyes. Eyes that belonged to a giant black wolf. The black wolf stared at Kayah briefly, then took off into the woods. Not wanting him to get away, she chased it. Shortly after she entered the woods, Kayah lost sight of the wolf. She closed her eyes, trying to sense the wolf's direction. She came up with nothing; the wolf was gone. The wolf watched as she searched the surrounding area and found no trace of him. When it was almost dawn, Kayah gave up searching and returned to Dezra's house; she wanted to shower before Dezra woke.

Just as Kayah turned the shower off, she heard Dezra shuffle from her room. Kayah opened the door as Dezra reached for the handle.

"Bitch, don't you ever sleep? You just scared the shit out of me." Dezra panted, grabbing her chest.

"Well, good morning to you, too. I am going to raid your closet for some clothes. "Go shower and get ready for work, and I will make you some breakfast," Kayah said sweetly.

Dezra pushed past her and yelled as she shut the bathroom

door, "Make sure you cook some cacoochie."

"Damn it, Dezra, that is not what it is called."

"Love you She-Bitch," was the last thing Kayah heard before the sound of water filled the air.

After they ate, Kayah cleaned up while Dezra finished preparing for work. Kayah grabbed the box with her father's leather as they left the house. The ride home was quiet, other than the radio playing softly. Kayah sighed when she saw Demon's truck in her driveway.

"Girl... he doesn't know when to quit, does he?"

"No," snarled Kayah.

She entered her house without looking at the truck and locked the door behind her. It wasn't long before the pounding on her door started.

"Kayah, come on, open the door. I know you are in there," Demon yelled.

After ten minutes, the pounding stopped, and she sat down to make a list of things she needed to do.

Kayah's to-do list

Stain the deck

paint the kitchen

paint the living room

finish remodeling the master bath

Search into my past

Travel to Baton Rouge

Find the remaining members of my father's pack

Reclaim my birthright.

Get justice for my parents.

Kayah lowered her head in defeat and said, "I know you are here, Demon. You might as well come and sit down instead of being a B and E creeper."

Demon slowly approached the corner from the living room and leaned on the door jam. She looked at him and asked, "If you were going to just come in anyway, why did you knock like an idiot for ten minutes?"

"I was hoping you would have invited me in and not be an asshat," smiled Demon.

"Do you think I wanted to see you? Your father is a prick, and you made an ass of yourself."

"I know my dad is a prick. So how did I make an ass out of myself?" he asked.

"You confessed your undying love for me, knowing we could never be mates, and I have already told you no."

Chapter 5

Demon chose not to fight with her and sat down at the table, "So what are you working on?" he asked as he grabbed her list to read it.

"A list of things I need to do?" she said calmly.

"If you wait until this weekend, I will go to Baton Rouge with you. Before you say...you don't need anyone to go with you, you will need someone there for moral support. Going back there will bring up a lot of bad memories."

Kayah sat back and looked at him; she knew he was right.

"Demon, you are right. I need someone to go with me. But it doesn't need to be you. I can get Dezra to go with me."

"Kayah, come on, think smart. You are going back to where your parents were killed. What if the Hunters catch wind that you are in town? I know you can take care of yourself, and so can Dezra, But I am bigger and stronger than her. Yes, I know you are much bigger and stronger than me with you being a Timberwolf."

"Demon, my parents were Timberwolves, and they killed them; it doesn't matter who I take. If they want me, they will come for me."

"Kayah, you know I love you. I have already told you that. I will not let anything happen to you."

"And that is the reason I don't want you to go. Not because you love me… it is because you can die. I could not handle if someone I care about dies because of me."

"You make no sense… you don't want to be with me. But you don't want me to go with you because I could die. And it is okay if Dezra goes, knowing damn well you would put your life on the line to save her."

She tipped her head and studied Demon, knowing he could see right through her bullshit reasons.

"Demon…"

"No! Just be quiet and let me finish. I know you love me as well. I felt it when I kissed you. I am going with you when you start looking for answers. I have a better chance of survival than Dezra does. Now if you want her to go, we can make it a double date and bring Shilo. Think about it, Kayah. As I said, be smart about this, there will be three of us to watch your back," Demon proposed.

The feeling of love overwhelmed Kayah, causing her eyes to fill; not wanting Demon to see her cry, she turned her head.

Demon carefully turned her face back and said softly, " No, Baby, don't hide from me. I love all the different pieces that make you. The strong, the weak, the bitchy, even the broken and shattered parts of you."

Kayah looked Demon in the eyes when he cupped her cheek for the first time. The love she saw in those gorgeous yellow eyes made the tears spill over.

"Baby, there is no need to cry. No matter how much you push me away, I am not going anywhere."

"Demon, the truth is I do love you. I love you so much that it hurts, and it feels like my heart will explode. But you and I could never be because of my bloodline, and you have been promised to another. So sometimes it is easier to push you away than let you stay near," Kayah said sadly.

"Why don't you let me worry about my father and the pack? So this is what I am going to do. Today I will tell work I will take a leave of absence for the rest of the month. Then tonight, I will cook dinner, and we can invite Dezra and Shilo over and devise a plan. How does that sound?" Demon asked.

She nodded, not knowing what to say; she asked, "Would you like some breakfast before you leave for work?"

Demon knew she was looking for something to do to put this emotional morning behind them. He nodded.

Kayah quickly grabbed the stuff to make a ham and cheese omelet. When it was done, she set the plate and a cup of orange juice before him. He ate a few bites and then asked, " So my father and I got into a huge fight last night. Can I crash on your couch until I find somewhere else?"

"Demon, you are playing with fire. If Colby finds out you are here, it is considered a betrayal; you could be tried for treason."

"Babe, I told you to let me worry about my father and the pack."

"No, you can not stay on my couch. However, I will clean the guest room; you can stay there," Kayah offered.

"Thank you. I will grab some of my stuff after I get out of work. Then I will stop at the store."

"I can go by the store and pick up stuff for dinner. What do you want to fix?" she asked.

Demon stood and grabbed his dishes; after putting them in the sink, he turned and looked at Kayah. "I'll send you a text after I talk to Shilo."

"Sounds good. I will text Dezra this morning."

Demon walked over to the kitchen door and jingled his keys, "What time are you going to be back here? I don't want to climb through your bedroom window again." asked Demon.

"What time do you get out of work? Plus, if you are staying here, I will get you a key made. This is not an invitation for you to move in. Got it?"

He nodded, "I will get off about five; after I go to my parent's house, I will be here about six."

"I will be here. I need to go out for a few things, but I will be back. I will wait until I get your text before leaving for town," she said.

He nodded once more and headed out the door. Kayah watched him climb into his truck and back down the driveway, wondering what kind of trouble she got into. She fixed a cup of coffee and took it outside to sit on her new deck. Once she was seated, she pulled out her phone and texted Dezra.

Kayah: *Girl, U busy?*

Dezra: *Nope, slow as shit here.*

Kayah: *U, Shilo my house, dinner.*

Dezra: *WTF????? What is going on?*

Kayah: *Bitch… Food…What do you want to eat?*

Dezra: *Shrimp and steak don't matter. U grillin'?*

Kayah: *Nope, Demon is.*

Dezra: *What U playing at?*

Kayah: *STFU. I need to talk to you tonight. I need a favor from you.*

Dezra: *For real?*

Kayah: *Yes!*

Dezra: *Girl! Did you fuck Demon?*

Kayah: *Girl... Boo. SMH... NO!!!!!*

Dezra: *K... see you tonight.*

Kayah: *Later!*

Kayah finished her cup of coffee and started staining the deck.

∞∞∞

As Demon drove to work, he replayed the morning events and smiled to himself, knowing that he was slowly breaking down the walls Kayah had built around herself for protection.

Pulling into the steel plant, he noticed Shilo was just parking. He pulled in next to his long-time friend and packmate, turned off the truck, and jumped out.

"Hey, my bro." Demon said as he grasped Shilo's hand and gave him a half hug in greeting.

"Hey D. What's up? Where have you been?" Shilo asked.

"Man," he said, shaking his head. "I don't have time to get into that. But I do need to ask you something. Can you come to dinner tonight over at Kayah's? Dezra will be there, and there is something we need to ask you?"

"What the fuck are you doing, man? Kayah is taboo; please tell me you are not sleeping with her. Don't get me wrong, she is an incredible chick and my girl's best friend... getting involved with her is asking for trouble," Shilo said, taking a step back.

"Man, is the only thing people look at is the wolf? My parents raised her, making her a part of this pack. Plus, she is your girl's best friend. She learned some stuff from her past last night and needs our help. So are you coming to dinner or not?" he asked.

"Fuck...fuck...fuck. Yes, I will be there. You know I got your back, no question. Tell me the truth. Are you in love with Kayah?"

"Yes, I have loved her since I was sixteen."

"Fuck, man, you are going to get us all killed. One more question what are you going to do about Taria?"

"What about her?" Demon asked.

"Where you hit on the head? When you become Alpha, she will be your mate and old lady."

"I will worry about that later. But, come on, we are going to be late," said Demon pulling out his vibrating phone.

Kai: *Dezra said yes to food. She wants shrimp and steak. Is that cool with you and Shilo?*

Demon: *Yes. Surf and Turf sound good. Pick up some red skins, greens, and some rolls.*

Kai: *Do you want some neck bones for the greens?*

Demon: *Is that a question?*

Kai: *Dick!!*

Demon: *Sorry just trying to lighten the mood.*

Kai: *U good. Anything else?*

Demon: *No, I will pick up a couple of bottles of wine.*

Kai: *K... Later!*

Demon: *Later*

Demon took one last look at his phone and shoved it back into his pocket. Then, he looked at Shilo and said, "We are having surf and turf for dinner. Can you and Dezra pick up a couple of bottles of red wine? Oh, and not the box stuff, either."

"Yes, We can do that," Shilo said before entering the building.

∞∞∞

When the work day was done, Demon and Shilo headed to their trucks. Shilo slowed, making Demon look back at him.

"Dude, what's up? Did you forget something?" Demon asked.

"No. Do you know that guy?"

"What guy?"

Shilo pointed, "The guy leaning up against your truck."

Demon turned and saw—a man with shoulder-length black hair and porcelain white skin. His eyes were yellow and red, and he wore a white shirt, jeans, and motorcycle boots.

"No. But I am going to find out who he is and why he is leaning on my truck," said Demon before walking to the stranger.

"Hey man, do you need something?" Shilo asked.

The stranger ignored Shilo and spoke to Demon, "I have a warning for you."

"Oh yeah, what's that?" Demon asked smugly.

"I came to warn you to stay away from Kayah."

Demon stiffened, "Who are you?"

"I am someone that has been watching Kayah since the night her parents were killed. I watch her every night when she tries to run the nightmares away. I am the one that is telling you that she is not the one for you. So stay away from her."

Demon sniffed the air but could not tell what the stranger was. "What are you?" Demon asked.

"I am the wolf that will lose its cool quickly if you don't heed my warning."

The stranger pushed off Demon's truck and walked to his Harley without saying anything. After he straddled his bike, he made eye contact with Demon and said, "If you are a smart man, you will heed my warning. Stay away from Kayah." Then he put on dark sunglasses and drove away.

"What the fuck, man. Who the hell was that?" asked Shilo.

"I don't know…but one thing I do know, I do not like how he has been watching Kayah. So I will find out who and what he is. And what the hell he wants with Kayah." Demon looked over at Shilo and said, "See you tonight."

Shilo nodded, got in his truck, and drove away. After Demon climbed into his truck, he pulled out his phone and texted to ensure she was okay.

Demon: *Kai, U okay?*

Kayah: *Yea, why wouldn't I be?*

Demon: *Just checking. Out of work and heading to my parent's house to grab some stuff, but I will be there soon.*

Kayah: *Okay, see you soon. Shopping is done, steak marinating, deck stained, and now I am cleaning the guest bedroom.*

Demon: *Don't work too hard. I can help when I get there.*

Kayah: *You are grilling the food. I will call Dezra and see if she can help.*

Demon: *Sounds good… Later.*

Kayah: *Later.*

Chapter 6

Kayah looked at the time and decided to call instead of texting.

"Hey, girl," answered Dezra.

"Hey, can you come over after work and help me with something?" asked Kayah.

"Sure, what are we doing?"

"I am cleaning out the guest room."

"Why are you cleaning it out? I thought you were working on remodeling your house."

"Demon got into a huge fight with Colby, so I am letting him stay here until he gets a place."

Dezra laughed, "Bitch you are letting him move in. You two do have a death wish."

"No. I am just helping him out," Kayah snapped.

"What will you do if Colby or Taria finds out?"

"What if they do? I am just letting him stay here until he gets his place. It's not like we are moving in together. I just figured the bed in the guest room would be more comfortable. I won't disturb him if I go on a night run," Kayah explained.

"You make a good case. Now let's see if others believe it. I will see you after work."

When Dezra disconnected, Kayah tossed her phone on the bed and picked up another box to take to the attic. She never noticed the wolf in the woods listening to every word she said. It wasn't long before Kayah heard Dezra come through the kitchen door.

"Go ahead and raid my closet and get out those scrubs," Kayah yelled.

"I planned on it," she yelled back.

After Dezra was changed, she joined Kayah in the guest bedroom, and together they carried the boxes to the attic. Kayah heard Demon's truck pull up as they were finishing with the last of the boxes.

"Kai, where are you at?"

"Back here, Demon," she yelled.

Demon followed her voice, but instead of finding Kayah, he found a ladder leading to a trap door in the ceiling.

"You still got a lot to move?" he yelled, looking up the latter to the attic.

Kayah poked her head in the opening, "Nope, that was the last of the boxes. If you give me a minute, I will help you bring your stuff in."

Demon turned and looked toward the kitchen, "I can get it. Shilo just got here, and he will help. But, you girls, be careful coming down the ladder."

Kayah gave him a brilliant smile, "10-4, good buddy." Then she disappeared into the attic.

Demon smiled and shook his head. Kayah and Dezra decided they had done enough work for the day, so they sat down at the kitchen table with a glass of peach Nehi. That is where Demon and Shilo found them twenty minutes later. Shilo bent to kiss

Dezra, and Demon plopped down in the chair beside Kayah.

Kayah looked at him, smiling big, and said, "Dinner? You are

the one that said you were cooking for this shindig."

"I said I was going to grill... I never said cook. Shilo and I can

grill, and you two can fix the sides. Then after we eat, we can

get down to the unpleasant."

"Sounds good."

Kayah looked at her friends before standing, knowing they

would pity her when they found out the truth. Dezra watched

Kayah as she finished fixing the sides for dinner and watched

the guys out the window and thought.

She knew Kayah was in love with Demon, the kind of love in all

caps. She looked out the window at the guys and could see just by

looking, the Alpha's son felt the same way. Yet, she felt torn; was

she to be loyal to her pack and report this to her Alpha? Or did she

stay true to the lifelong friend that became her family? She wished

she felt that way about Shilo. It never set right with Dezra that her love life was decided for her when she was born. She liked him well enough and hoped one day, love would grow, but it felt forced. She caught Demon looking up at the window. Was he hoping Kayah was simultaneously looking out the window to steal a hiding glance they only shared?

"Girl, You can lie to everyone else, but you can not lie; you are in love with that wolf," Dezra said softly.

"Dezra, I fell in love with Demon a long time ago. It was the night of my sixteenth birthday."

"That was the first night you started running at night."

"Yes, he saw when I snuck out my bedroom window and shifted. I sensed him following me; knowing I wasn't alone was comforting. He ran with me all night, and when we returned, he never asked any questions, but the most significant thing was he kept my running at night a secret. He could have told Colby and Chloe, but he didn't. So you are the only one that knows when I started running, and that is because I am the one that told you," she said without looking at her friend.

"Does he still run with you now?" she asked.

"He quit for a while but has been running with me lately."

"Why did he stop?"

"Because I have been a bitch to him. Whenever he started getting too close, I would push him away. Because I knew if I let him get too close, my heart would shatter when he married Taria."

"You know there will be hell to pay if you two go against the pack's law," Dezra warned.

"So what are you going to do? By pack law, you are duty-bound to turn what I have told you tonight over to your Alpha," Kayah asked.

"Girl, you know that I am on your side. If you are going to start a war because you are in love with a man, there is no drought that I will always have your back," Dezra stated proudly.

"I just hope Shilo feels the same way."

"One question, though?"

"What?" Kayah asked as she carried the food to the table.

"What are you going to do about Taria?"

"Oh... I forgot about that bitch," Kayah snarled as she went to the window and yelled at the guys.

After everyone ate and the kitchen was cleaned, they took their drink to the living room for an unpleasant conversation. Kayah and Dezra curled up on opposite ends of the couch, and the guys took the other two chairs. Demon looked at Kayah and asked, "Do you want me to start?"

Kayah nodded and took a deep drink of red wine.

"Kayah and I asked you guys over here because you are our closest friends, and we need your help. First, let me say I am in love with Kayah, and I don't give a shit if you disapprove. Second, Kayah found out some information yesterday from Colby. As you know, Kayah is a Timberwolf, and her parents were killed, and my father was friends with her father. So when they were murdered, my father took her in and raised her. What was kept from us is that her father was an Alpha. Colby told Kayah never to tell anyone that her father was the Alpha of the Baton Rouge New Moon Chapter. Nyko and Ashseara were her parents. Kayah is not a Beta wolf; she is the first Omega born in centuries. Kayah is from one of the ancient five bloodlines. On her twenty-first birthday, she will ascend into her full powers."

"Holy fuck, brother. Why was this kept from the pack and us? If Colby had told the pack this, Kayah would have been welcomed?" asked Shilo.

"Because the men that murdered my parents are still looking for me. The night they died, I saw everything," Kayah said.

"What do you mean you saw everything?" Shilo asked.

"I watched in horror when each one of the bastards took their turn raping and torturing my mother while making my father watch. Then I watched as they executed my parents —one bullet to each of their heads. All because of me. They wanted me because of my bloodline. On my birthday, I will be an Alpha. Plus, if they forced me to mate with their male wolves, my children would have my power making their bloodline stronger," explained Kayah.

"Kayah, that means you are not a Timberwolf… you are a werewolf," Shilo said, standing so he could pace.

"Is it true that whoever you mate with your pups will have werewolf traits?" asked Dezra.

"If the lore is actual, then yes," said Kayah.

"Holy fuck. Colby is a dick. No offense, Demon," Shilo said.

"No offense taken, but what made you say that?"

"Think about it. You are in line to be Alpha, and if Kayah were a part of this pack, you would have a right to take her as a mate. I have concluded that Kayah would overtake his pack because she will be a more powerful Alpha than you," explained Shilo.

"That makes a lot of sense," said Demon.

Shilo stood behind Dezra, placed his hands on her shoulders, and said, "We are in one hundred percent. We will keep your secrets, including if you two pursue being mates. But, Kayah, I am sorry for my part in growing up and making you an outcast. We were raised what our Alpha said was law. Now, what do you need our help with?"

Kayah covered her face and wept; she never expected to be accepted for who she was. Instead, all her life, she was treated as an outcast. It was almost too much to handle. Pulling herself together, she wiped her eyes and said, "I will seek out the truth. I will get justice for my parents. Demon and I are headed to Baton Rouge, and Demon thinks it will be safer if we go as a group. I will find out if members of my wolf pack are still alive. If they are, I am going to bring them back together. Plus, I want to rebuild my father's MC chapter. I know you have loyalty to Colby. All I am asking is to help watch our backs."

Shilo nodded and looked at Demon, "Since we are bringing things out in the open. Demon, have you told Kayah about the visitor that was waiting for you today?"

"What visitor, Demon?" Kayah asked.

"I was going to tell you about it tonight, I promise. But this guy was leaning on my truck when I left work today. He said he was a wolf, and he said he had a warning for me. I think he was lying. He did not smell like a wolf, and he was not human," said Demon.

"The fucking weird part was his eyes. They were yellow and red," Shilo chimed in.

"What was the...Wait what...Did you say his eyes were yellow and red?" asked Kayah.

"Yes...what's up Kayah?" asked Demon.

"If it is the same person, he was telling the truth. He is a wolf. But you are right. He doesn't smell like one," she said.

"When did you see him?"

"Well, I didn't see him technically. However, when I left your parent's house last night, I saw these yellow and red orbs in the woods. Then when I woke up from the nightmare, he was in the woods outside Dezra's house. So I went after him, but he disappeared. So I know he is a black wolf with yellow and red eyes. And before you bitch at me, he was huge. So I was hoping it was someone from my father's pack. What was the warning he had for you?"

"He told me if I knew what was best for me, I would stay away from you," Demon said, crossing his arms.

"I don't like it...plus he said he had been watching you since the night your parents were killed," Shilo added.

"You mean he was there the night my parents were killed? What did he look like? Maybe he is one of the ones that killed my parents," panted Kayah.

"I don't think he is, Kayah," Demon said carefully.

"How would you know you weren't there that night?"

"Kayah, think about it. He said he has been watching you since then. The Hunters murdered your parents because they would not give you up. If this mystery wolf were part of The Hunters' pack, don't you think he would have told the others about you?" he explained.

"Okay, so if he was not one of the guys, who is he? Did he tell you his name?" asked Kayah.

"He would not tell us his name. I think he thinks he is your protector," Shilo chimed in.

"Well, I say we put him on the list of things we need to figure out. Kayah, what do you want to do first?" asked Dezra.

"I say we play it by ear. If I want answers to my past, I need to go home. When can you all get the time off work? I already have time off. Today was the first official day my vacation started."

"I told work that I needed a leave of absence effective immediately. But, Shilo, I informed the boss that you might call and ask for the same."

"I have about two months of paid time off I can take. I have already sent a message to Sandra in HR. I am just waiting on a text back," Dezra added.

Chapter 7

While waiting for Dezra to get a callback, they sat silently to their thoughts. Kayah looked at the people willing to put their lives on the line to help her. Dezra was doing something on her phone with a look of concentration.

Dezra~ *I hope Kayah knows my views have shifted. I am loyal to her, but my opinions have moved from the pack. Or should I say the Alpha of the pack? I don't trust Colby. Why would he keep this from the pack? If the pack had known the truth years ago, they would have helped protect her and help find her answers. I know I can't make up for the past, but maybe I can help her by finding a place we can start looking for the answers.*

Kayah wished she could take the guilt she knew her best friend had. But, now she knew there was no blame to place on the pack. They followed their Alpha faithfully. The chiming sound of Shilo's phone caused her to gaze in his direction.

Shilo~ *Rock on this is good news. I hope this information will help us find some of Nyko's pack still alive. Timberwolves are very territorial; I hope they see us as friends instead of rivals. Also, I wonder if anyone knows what happened to Kayah that night. Fuck she was just a baby when her parents were killed. I wonder if Demon could challenge Colby for leadership. That's touchy ground... could Colby be brought up on treason charges himself? I have my suspicions about why Colby kept this a secret. One thing I am sure about Colby's actions caused Kayah to grow up in a group of wolves that would have seen her as family; it would not have mattered that she is a Timberwolf. Demon could choose her as his mate if she were a pack member, breaking no-pack laws.*

Shilo noticed Kayah was watching him; he offered her a soft smile. She smiled back and looked at the man for whom she would crawl through hell.

Demon~ *I wonder if the mystery wolf is Kaya's mate from the Timberwolf pack? If he is, he has another thing coming. If he is part of the pack she is seeking, why has he taken so long to make*

himself known? I must be careful moving forward from here with

Kayah and the pack. My father will be one of the biggest obstacles

to overcome. But I love her and will do anything I need to protect

the woman who will be my lifelong mate.

Kayah got lost in her thoughts. The last couple of days has

her in a whirlwind. But then, the wrapping on the door pulled

her out of the cycle of thoughts.

"Girl, who the fuck is coming over here this late?" Dezra

asked.

"I don't fucking know...my luck, the world is about to start

falling because it is Colby, and he found out that Demon is

staying in my guest room," Kayah said as she stomped off.

Kayah was scowling when she opened the door to find Taria

on the other side. Taria was pretty until her attitude started to

show. Taria was one of the popular girls in school that always

looked down on Kayah because she was a Timberwolf. She was

a tall blonde with sky-blue eyes. Kayah would describe her as statuesque, and the worst part is she was promised to Demon.

"Is there a reason you are knocking on my door?" asked Kayah.

"I need to talk to Demon," snapped Taria.

"First of all, you can change how you talk to me. This is my goddamn house," Kayah said before yelling for Demon.

"Demon, there is someone here to see you."

"Who is it, Kai?" asked Demon.

"Taria," she said as she leaned her shoulder in the door jam.

"What? Why the fuck is she here?" Demon asked, walking into the kitchen.

"Demon, Baby, I have been looking for you everywhere," Taria said as she wrapped her arms around his neck, trying to kiss him.

Demon gripped her arms and gently pushed her back, creating distance between them.

"Why are you here, Taria?" Demon asked again.

"Can we go talk?" she asked.

"No, say what you need to say."

"Baby, please. Do we have to talk in front of her? She isn't part of this pack. She was branded as an outcast when she was little."

"Did you forget you are standing on my deck at my house?" asked Kayah.

"I am only going to ask again. What the fuck do you want, Taria?"

"Well, I went by your house, and Colby said you had moved out. So I went looking for you. I wanted to tell you that you can move in with me. It is an excellent time to take our relationship to the next level. We can plan our wedding for the beginning of fall."

"Taria, are you fucking delusional? What in your right mind would make you think that would be okay? I have never spent time with you. I have never kissed you. Plus, I have told you multiple times that I have no interest in you."

"But you are my mate. Demon, we are fated," she said,

pushing out her bottom lip, trying to be cute.

"I will tell you this one last time as nicely as possible. I am not your mate, nor will I ever be. You are gorgeous, but your attitude makes you ugly." Demon explained.

"But you are in line to be Alpha, and your mate was chosen for you when you were born. So you will never become Alpha if we don't wed," Taria growled.

"I don't care," snapped Demon.

"So, you have talked to Demon. Now you can leave," Kayah said.

Shilo and Dezra wanted to know what was taking so long, so they decided to find out. So they came and stood behind Kayah and Demon.

"What brings prom queen here?" sneered Dezra.

"I came to collect my mate," she answered primly.

"You are truly dense, Demon just told you how he felt, but you are too stupid to comprehend," Kayah laughed.

Kayah watched as Taria's body stiffened and her fingers curled into fists.

"This is pack business, but you wouldn't know anything about that. The pack treats you as an outcast, and you grew up in the Alpha's house; now that is bad. When will you catch on that you are not wanted? Your parents died to get away from you. You are just a sad, poor excuse of a wolf," Taria smirked, knowing what she said landed just the way she wanted.

"Back off, Taria. You are talking about things you have no idea about," Shilo warned.

"Since when did you start sticking up for this freak?" Taria snapped.

The only notice that Taria got that something was off

was when Kayah's eyes started to glow. But then, the Alpha animalistic rage took over, and Kayah attacked. When Kayah's fist connected with Taria's face, her head snapped back.

"Now, that is our last warning. Keep your mouth shut and get the fuck off my property. Next time, no warning will be given; I will tear you from limb to limb."

"If you were smart, you would leave," Shilo added.

"What is wrong with you guys? She's not even a wolf. Her eyes are glowing like a freak. Demon, please come with me," Taria pleaded.

"You need to realize there is nothing here for you. To educate you, Kayah is a wolf. She is a Timberwolf, an Alpha, to be exact. Now I would leave before my girl wolfs out and tears you apart," Dezra smiled, showing her k-9's

"You don't believe this bullshit, do you?" she asked, looking at Demon.

"It's all true, Taria. If you don't believe me, ask your Alpha for the truth," he said.

"Don't you mean your father?"

"NO! I meant what I said. GO ASK YOUR ALPHA!" barked Demon.

Tears started to form in Taria's eyes. Then, with one last look at the group, she said. "You all will regret this."

Then Taria jogged down the deck's stairs, ran to her car, and sped away.

∞∞∞

The wolf in the woods was impressed with how the Dire wolves came to Kayah's defense. The arrogant wolf may be a good mate for Kayah. He would need to watch him closely before making up his mind. But for now, he needed to watch the others that meant to harm Kayah. So the wolf took off toward the Dire wolf Alpha's house.

Taira beat her hands on the steering wheel of the car from anger. She knew it would not end well when Colby called and asked her to come by. She never slowed down when she turned into the driveway, forcing her to slam on the brakes at the last minute missing Colby's bike by inches. She slammed the car door and stomped to the door. With tears streaming down her face, she beat her fist on the door. She was relieved when Colby answered the door himself.

"I am sorry I failed," she wailed.

"Come in and tell me what happened," Colby crooned while wrapping an arm around her.

When they were seated, she told him everything.

"Demon said that he will never be my mate, that he would rather be a lone wolf than marry me. Plus, they told me some crazy bullshit."

"What did they say, Taria?" asked Colby in a weary tone.

"That she is not only a Timberwolf but also an Alpha. That would make her Nyko's missing daughter."

"It is true she is the daughter of the Timberwolf Alpha. She is an Alpha by blood," Colby said quietly.

"If all that is true, Demon has the right to choose her as a mate. By pack law, the next in line to be Alpha has the right to select someone other than his arranged match if the other of his choosing is an Alpha from another pack. If all this is true, you kept this from the pack."

"Yes, I kept some of the information from the pack. But it was only to protect her. That is why I never made her submit to the pack; she has her own pack waiting for her to pick up the pieces. Demon will be your mate; he will submit and obey his Alpha. He is next in line to take over the pack. He will not walk away from that."

"But what you don't understand he has already walked away. He told me to talk to MY Alpha. I may still have time to sway him, but he is just trying to help his friend right now."

"Kayah is more than a friend to him. He told me last night he had been in love with her for years. I hope you are right, little wolf, because if you're wrong...the pack will have no more use for you."

The look in Colby's eyes sent fear skittering up her spine.

∞∞∞

Kayah and the others were working on a plan of action late into the night, so Dezra and Shilo decided to go home, pack some stuff and camp out at Kayah's. Kayah fell asleep, curled up in the chair, watching a movie with Demon. When she whimpered in her sleep, Demon looked at her from where he sat on the couch. He knew the nightmare had returned once again. Demon hoped the nightmare would start to fade once they started finding answers. He opened his mouth to call out her name. When her eyes opened, they looked wild and feral once again. After she blinked, Demon noticed they now looked haunted.

"Come on, Kai, let's go for a run," Demon suggested knowing that was the only thing that beat back the nightmare's grip.

She gave him a sad smile and headed to the kitchen door. Shilo's truck pulled in when Kayah and Demon stepped onto the porch. Not knowing what to do, Kayah thrust her hands into her pockets.

Dezra could see the need to run on her friend's face when she climbed out of the truck; she said, "Hey girl, are you going for a run?"

This time when she smiled, it made her eyes twinkle in the moonlight. "Yea, you know how much I love to run, but I just feel free when I run at night."

"It has been a long time since I got to run in the moonlight; I think I will join you," Dezra said, taking off her shirt.

"I would love for you to join me," said Kayah as she tossed her shirt on the ground.

"A run sounds fun. The last time I ran at night was when I was a teen. So I think I will go as well," Shilo added.

"Well, come on, everyone, we are wasting the moonlight. Let's run," Demon said, stripping.

As they all shifted, Kayah didn't know how to feel; she was never allowed to run with the pack. Instead, she was forced to stay at the clubhouse when the pack met once a month to run under the full moon.

As Kayah and the others ran and played like pups, they were unaware others were watching them. Taria watched how the others reacted around the female Alpha. She also noticed that Kayah's fur was almost pure white. She swore that Kayah was gray and white when they were younger when she saw her as a wolf. She started to believe that Colby was being truthful. Over the next few days, she would also be doing a little research. Taria was unaware she was walking a very thin line. The wolf that stayed in the shadows was watching her closely. If she harmed Kayah in any way, she would be his next meal.

Chapter 8

Early the following morning, Kayah noticed no awkwardness between her and Shilo; they had been friends for years. So they decided to take both trucks to make travel easier and more comfortable. She looked at her house and hopped in the truck with Demon. They agreed that Demon and Kayah would take the lead, and their first stop would be for breakfast once they were out of New Orleans. But before they could get on the road, they needed to deal with the person blocking the end of her driveway.

Colby and Sid blocked the end of the driveway with their bikes.

"Don't worry, Kayah, I will deal with this," Demon said with a hint of anger.

"We will deal with it together," she said as she jumped out of the truck.

Kayah walked down to the end of her driveway and said, "Good morning, Colby. Why are you here?"

"Well, we ended our conversation badly the other night."

"Dad, you are lying again. You did not bring Sid here to apologize to Kayah."

"You're right, son. I asked Sid to come and tell Kayah what he had witnessed that night. I made him swear to keep that night silent for your protection, Kayah."

Kayah studied Colby and saw he was telling the truth for once. She nodded and said, "Bring your bikes up to the house, and we can go inside, and you can tell all of us."

"I will tell Shilo and Dezra to join us in the house," said Demon.

Demon watched Kayah as she waited for Colby and Sid on the deck, so he quickly had the others join them in the house and went to join Kayah on the deck. However, Demon did not trust his father at all. In the house, Kayah paced. She had to relive that night again. Would she ever be able to put that night behind her?

Kayah stopped and gripped the back of the couch without looking up, "Go ahead, Sid. What do you need to tell me?"

"I would like to say I am sorry, Kayah. No one should ever go through what you did, and I am so sorry now that I am making you relive it again."

Kayah looked up, and when she looked at Sid, her eyes were glowing slightly, "I relive it every night in my sleep. The only thing that chases it away for a little while is when I run. It is the only time I am free from the horrors of that night."

"I think I can explain why when you run you feel free," Sid said.

"The night your parents were killed, how much do you remember after the Hunters left?" Sid asked.

She paused just a minute to think, "Nothing. The last thing I remember was my father getting shot."

"When Colby and I arrived at your house, we found you

lying across your parent's laps covered in blood. Kayah, you were in wolf form," explained Sid.

"How, she was just a child?" Demon asked.

"It is because of a couple of things. One is because of her bloodline, and she was shocked by what she saw," Colby explained.

"We vowed to protect you no matter what. When I tried to pick you up, you bit me and scared my arm," Sid said, pushing up his sleeve to show the scar.

"I was the only one that you would let near you. So I picked you up, sat on the porch swing, rocked you to sleep, and waited for Chloe to arrive. She took you home, cleaned you up, and sat with you until you could shift back. We kept you a secret as long as we could. The more people who knew your story, the more danger you were in. Chloe and I always wanted another child, so we told everyone we took in an orphaned pup, and you were now Demon's little sister," Colby explained.

"Is that the whole truth, Colby? Or are you hiding more

secrets?" asked Kayah.

"When your parent's house went up for sale, Colby and I went in together and bought it," said Sid holding the keys to the house out for Kayah to take.

Demon knew by the look on his father's face he was still hiding something. "I know there is something else you are not telling her. The secrets end here, and if you genuinely want Kayah to have peace with her past, you need to tell her everything. Please, father, help us. Don't hinder us," Demon pleaded.

Colby sat down feeling defeated; he knew the following words would change everything. He looked at Kayah and said, "As you know, Nyko and I were good friends. He was like a brother to me. So when your parents decided they couldn't wait to be married, I helped them keep the secret that they had jumped the broom."

"What does jumping the broom mean?" asked Kayah.

Colby smiled, "Your parents could not wait to sleep together.

I've never seen anyone love each other more than your parents did. Well, your mom ended up pregnant, and when they found out, they married before she started showing. Months later, your mom gave birth to a beautiful baby boy. Your father named him Onyx; your father knew right away he had the traits of the ancient bloodline. Your parents were so proud, and word about your brother spread quickly. We would bring the packs together one night a month and run under the full moon. Then, when your brother was four, he shifted for the first time. The pack gathered to run, and the Alpha of the gray wolves showed up and offered his daughter as a mate to Onyx to combine the two packs. Nyko turned him down because they were untrustworthy, and their club was into running guns and drugs. He told Nyko that he had made a very powerful enemy. Shortly after that, your brother went missing; he was never found. Six years later, Chloe and I were blessed with our child, and Demon was born. A year after that, you were born, and you were your daddy's princess. He told me that he loved you so much it hurt.

When we would get the packs together or if we just got together for a cookout, you and Demon were inseparable. So a few nights before your second birthday Nyko and I made a pact that you and Demon would be mates. You two would be the bridge that merged our packs; together, you would run the pack and the clubs. Then, the night your parents were killed, I had to break the pact we had made. We felt you were like your brother and were afraid you would fall to the same fate as Onyx. So I lied to the pack about where I found you and made a new pact about who would be Demon's mate. I had to make everyone think you were killed along with your parents." He looked Demon. "Son, Kayah is your true mate. I am so sorry."

When Colby was done talking, it was so quiet if a pin dropped, it would sound like a bomb had exploded.

"So, you are telling us that Kayah will be our Alpha?" asked Dezra.

"Was...Dezra, was," said Kayah.

"You're telling me that the woman I love was always meant to be my mate. And you telling me that you forbid me to be with her was to save fucking face because you lied?" growled Demon.

"I am telling you, she can still be your mate if she is brave enough to take back her title as Alpha of the Timberwolves," stated Colby.

Kayah looked at him with tear-filled angry eyes, "Why? Why tell me this now?" she asked.

"Because your birthday is in a few days, you will ascend to your full power and become a true Alpha. When you become an Alpha, you have a birthright claim on your father's pack and the MC. You must be careful before your birthday; you are just an Omega Timberwolf, but you will be a werewolf Alpha after your birthday. Therefore, I give you my full blessing to be mated to each other. You may only wed and make the unbreakable par bond between you after her birthday if you do it before she does not ascend. If she does not ascend, she will never be an Alpha. Because of the danger, will you please wait to go on your trip until after your birthday? I am not asking as an Alpha but as your father's best friend and the man who raised you as his own."

"If we are to wait, you will set a pack meeting and explain to the pack everything. Kayah deserves the pack's protection until her birthday. She should also have access to the pack's resources," demanded Demon.

"I agree with Demon on this, Kayah; by using pack resources, we can send pack members to find the Timberwolves and bring them here. That will take a few days. By the time they arrive, you will have ascended," Shilo added.

"You all are doing it again... you are making plans and not asking the one person how she feels about it. So, Kayah, how do you feel about all of this?" Dezra asked.

"The pack has never excepted me growing up; what makes you all think they will accept and help me now?" she asked.

"Because I am their Alpha. I will tell them that you and

Demon are their Alpha, and once you are wed, I will step down."

Kayah looked over at Demon, and for once, she let her emotions fly. She leaped over the back of the couch at Demon catching him off guard and making him stumble. "I agree we will wait here for my father's pack to come to us," she said with her head buried in his neck.

"Happy…Happy…Joy…Joy. You two no longer have to hide your relationship. But I still have one question. What are you all gonna do about Taria? Prom Queen, that spoiled rotten ass heftier, grew up thinking she was Demon's mate. She thinks she will be the Queen of this pack," Dezra asked.

"I will take care of it," said Colby.

"NO! I will take care of it. She has bullied me for the last time. What she said to me last night was the last straw. It would be my great pleasure to clear up this misunderstanding," said Kayah with a devious smile.

The rest of the day was like a whirlwind; Colby and Sid helped them unpack the trucks and repack them with the rest of Demon's stuff from Colby's house. Kayah felt part of a real family for the first time. Chloe and Petra (Sid's old lady) were cooking up a storm in her kitchen while everyone was moving Demon into her house. Now that she would be sharing a room with Demon and her guest bedroom was free, Dezra and Shilo decided to stay until everything was settled and done.

The wolf in the woods heard and saw everything that had happened, and he did not know what to think about the arrogant wolf being her mate. But he was happy that there would be more people to protect his precious Kayah until her birthday. It was a good idea to bring the Timberwolves down here; there would be less chance for The Hunters to find out where Kayah was. Her birthday was only a few days off, and everything would change. The closer her birthday got, the stronger the pull he felt toward her. He figured Colby would call a pack meeting with the Dire Wolves before the Timberwolves arrived to explain everything. That would help in two ways: more protection for Kayah and gathering the Timberwolves. He knew when Nyko was killed, the Timberwolves scattered, and he had also heard rumors that they were just waiting for the day their Alpha would call them back together. Kayah had already received her father's leather. Now all she needed was his bike. When he returned to the house after all the wolves were gone, he searched for the keys but never found them. That was one thing on his list he would check off; he would be the one to give her Nyko's bike and his club.

Chapter 9

Over the next couple of days, Kayah, Demon, Shilo, and Dezra worked on Kayah's to-do list for her house. Demon still slept in the living room even after moving all of his stuff into Kayah's room; they decided not to tempt fate by sleeping in the same bed before her birthday. And every night, when the nightmare returned, they ran with her as a pack. The wolf that watched from the shadows knew he needed to meet Kayah soon but backed off for now, knowing she was protected and he could help her in other ways. So trusting she was covered, he headed to work on his checklist.

Kayah heard the rumble of Colby's bike pulling in the day before her birthday. She poured him a cup of coffee and met him on the deck.

"Good morning Colby," she said, handing him the cup and

sitting down.

They sat in the morning silence, watching the sunrise and drinking coffee. Finally, when the sun peeked through the trees, Colby spoke, "I have called a pack meeting tonight at seven. Make sure you and Demon are there by six forty-five."

"Why do we need to be there early?" she asked.

"Because the Alpha of the pack is having you initiated into the pack. Then it will be announced who you are, and then tell the pack about our engagement," Demon said, bending down to kiss her.

"Oh…" was all she said.

"Dad can I ask you a question?" Demon asked.

"Of course son, you can ask me anything."

"If Kayah, was always ment to be my mate who was Tiara ment to be with?"

"Originally the only arranged mates were ment for Alpha's. But since we needed to hide Kayah we mated all the pups. That will tell every one about the mating tonight when I explain everything else," Colby explained.

"How are the mated wolves going to handle that? Knowing that they were not fated." ask Kayah.

"All of the wolves that were mated, none of them have been par bonded. So they choose to be together or with someone of their choosing," Colby stated.

Colby knew that Kayah and Demon had a lot to talk about, plus he had thing to prepare for the pack meeting. After Colby's bike rumbled to life he nodded at the future of his pack and drove off.

Over the next few hours Demon helped Kayah finish painting the kitchen. When she was distracted by Dezra he slipped off to make a few phone calls.

"I found out this morning from Colby that the pairing up the pup when they are born was created when I needed to go into hiding."

"What? Does this mean Shilo and I don't have to be mated?" Dezra asked.

"Yes, that is exactly what I mean. Colby is going to announce it to the pack tonight." Kayah said looking up to find Dezra staring over her shoulder. "What is wrong?"

"Not to freak you out but there is a Gray wolf standing just in the clearing by the woods we run," Dezra said with little shake to her voice.

Kayah turned just in time to see the wolf dart back into the swampy woods. Kayah ran from the room and searched for Demon. She found Shilo and Demon siting on the deck out front, she stopped in front of Demon panting from trying to fend off the panic attack.

Demon was instantly rattled by the look on her face,"Kai, Baby, what's wrong," he asked.

"I think they have found me," she said before Dezra cut her off.

"What she is not telling you is there was a Gray wolf watching us through the window," she blurted out.

"Where?" Demon growled.

"Out back just outside the woods we run," Dezra said.

With out saying anything Shilo and Demon took off shifting as they ran leaving ripped and torn clothes behind them. Demon found the sent of the gray wolf relatively quick. Shilo stopped after they followed the sent for a while , "Demon we need to go back, if this is the pack that is responsible for the death of Kayah's parents this could be a trap. We need to get back, the girls were left unprotected."

Demon nodded and ran back to the house as fast as he could. They returned to find Kayah's house ransacked and the girls were missing. As they pulled on fresh clothes they sniffed the air.

"I smell the girls and the sent of the gray wolf," said Shilo.

"Same here, the smell of the intruder is fading, but the sent of the girls is still strong. They are still in the house," Demon said searching.

Demon walked through the house every so often sniffing the air, when he reach the hallway he looked up, "Baby, its me you can come down now. The coast is clear."

Slowly the hatch to the attic opened and the ladder extended. The first to poke her head out was Dezra, "All clear?"

"Yes, all clear," Demon said."

"Good, this dumb white she-bitch wanted to go after the damn cockbibber. I had to drag her stubborn ass and push her up the fuckin ladder. I am glad she is your mate and just my best friend. I think she is just as hard headed as you are. If she was my damn mate I would give her a whoopin. Going after a damn wolf she thinks is a murderer," Dezra ranted.

Kayah shook her head, "Dezra, shut your face."

"No. YOU listen to me damn it. Do you have a damn death wish? Kayah, you ascend tonight at midnight. I will personally help you track down and kill every last one of them fuckers. But not until it is safe for you. Stop acting on human emotions. You need to think and plan like a wolf. Please be smart, I would lose my shit if anything ever happened to you."

Knowing Dezra was right all Kayah did was nod and hug her

friend.

"The house has been compromised, we need a new place to lay low until Kayah ascends into her full powers," suggested Shilo.

"We can head to the club house. There is only a couple hours before the pack meeting starts. Kayah, make sure you bring a change of clothes. Shilo, stay with the girls while I call my father and tell him what happened so he can make sure there is enough security for tonight," Demon said as he walked into the livingroom.

"Why would I need a change of clothes?," she asked.

"Because, when you ascend it will force you to shift. And you will not have time to remove clothes or control it. When you ascend you will become a werewolf and with it being a full moon you will have no control over anything. Or the legend says," Shilo shrugged.

"I guess you don't need cloths if you want to run around showing you titties and kitty off," added Dezra.

"Bitch, I can't fuckin stand your ass right now," Kayah said stomping off to her room, with Dezra laughing behind her.

$$\infty \infty \infty$$

Thirty minutes later both trucks pulled into the club house and noticed Colby and Sid were already there. Colby met them and opened the truck door for Kayah. When she stepped out of the truck he enveloped her in a hug, "Kayah, are you okay? If you see him again would you recognize him? How bad was the house damaged?" he asked.

"Colby, I'm fine. Yes, I think I would recognize him. The house is just a mess, I think he was just checking to see if it was me."

"Well thank god you are okay. WHAT THE FUCK WERE YOU THINKING GIRL! I TOLD YOU HOW IMPORTANT IT WAS YOU STAYED SAFE UNTIL YOU ASCEND," he said as he shook her.

"Dad, stop shaking her. She is okay, and she learned her lesson," Demon said grabbing a hold of Colby's arm.

"You two truly are mates. Thick headed as bulls...the both of you. Come on lets go in. Your mother has been wanting to talk to you."

"He means you, Demon."

"Umm. He means the both of us. After tonight she will be your mother too, sweetheart," Demon said with a smile.

"Well, fuck," was all Kayah said before she walked to the clubhouse.

∞∞∞

Kayah had no idea the Dire Wolf pack was so big. She remembered growing up anywhere from fifteen to twenty pack members that would attend the meetings. There were over two hundred and fifty wolves, the ages ranged from newborn to the oldest member at a hundred and twenty-five. This was the Full Moon chapter, from what she understood there were other Dire Wolf packs in Mississippi, Alabama, Texas, and some could be found in the northern states. But the southern states were the biggest packs in the United States. The pack meeting never bothered her before, but now she would stand in front of the pack and take the Dire Wolf law as part of her own making her a part of the pack. Demon poked her in the side before she could wander into her own thoughts.

It begins~

Colby: *Wolves of the Full Moon, I call this meeting to order.*

All wolves: *Yes, Alpha.*

Colby: *I have called you here for a couple of things. First on the list is to explain some things that need to be said. Kayah will you join me?*

Kayah: *Yes, Colby.*

Colby: *Do you all remember when I took in this orphaned pup?*

All wolves: *Yes, Alpha.*

Colby: *Now is the time to tell you how she became my ward and who she truly is. The reason this was kept from you was for her safety. This wolf is Kayah, daughter of Nyko of the New Moon Timberwolves. Tonight we welcome her into our pack, you all will* *welcome her as one of your own. You will protect her as one of your own. You will run and hunt with her as one of your own. As your Alpha you will submit and obey these commands.*

All wolves: *Yes, Alpha!*

Colby: *Kayah, do you take our laws as your own?*

Kayah: *Yes!*

Colby: *Will you submit and obey me as your Alpha?*

Kayah: *Yes, Alpha.*

Then to show her submission Kayah dropped to all fours.

Colby: *Kayah, as your Alpha I welcome you to this pack, but do not require you to turn your back on yours. I will allow you to be duty bound to both of the laws of the packs. You may stand.*

Kayah stood and looked at the man that raised her, soon he would be her father as well.

Colby: *Kayah, welcome to the Full Moon wolf pack.*

Kayah's right shoulder blade started to burn, pulling off her shirt she looked back and saw the Dire wolf mark under the Timberwolf mark she had been born with. She didn't care she was standing in front of the wolves in her pants and bra, she was proud to finally belong.

Colby: *Second order of business. All arranged matches have here by been dissolved. The reason they were created in the first place was to keep Kayah hidden and safe. The only arranged match will be Demon and Kayah. The match was made after Kayah was born by Nyko and myself. Last order of business is tonight at midnight Kayah will turn twenty-one. Kayah is not a Beta wolf she is an Omega born into an Alpha's bloodline. When Kayah ascends she will be the Alpha of the Timberwolves New Moon chapter. With the union of Demon and Kayah we will combine our packs. When they are wed I will step down and they will be your Alpha's. Do any of you have something to say?*

Taria: *So this means I don't have to marry Demon?*

Colby: *No, you may marry someone of your choosing.*

Taria squealed and pushed everyone out of her way; when she was close enough, Taria jumped in Shilo's arms.

"Oh, thank the lord. I bless this union," yelled Dezra making

Kayah snort.

Colby: *I am going to bring this business to close but the meeting is not over. If everyone is agreeable on tonight's business, then I hear call business closed.*

All wolves: *Yes, Alpha.*

As the night went on Kayah was greeted by wolves she grew up with and some she had never met. They all treated her like family, she was now one of them. The next part would be harder, after she ascends she would take the lead on her father's pack.

When it was close to midnight they all went outside under the full moon. Kayah felt when the change started. Out of a clear sky clouds covered the moon and Kayah screamed in pain. She fell to all fours and her bones started to shift ripping the clothes from her body. When Kayah was in wolf form her body started changing again, her eyes glowed a brilliant blue and her fur was white as fresh fallen snow. Her bones stretched and her canines grew, as a Timberwolf she was bigger than the rest of the Dire Wolves, now she was three times her normal size. When the clouds moved to reveal the moon she tipped her head back and howled for the first time as an Alpha. This caused the pack to shift, when Demon was at her side she ran for the first time with a real pack.

The wolf from the shadows was rounding up Timberwolves when he heard the howl. It was like the night when Kayah's parents were killed, but this time he was in human form. He looked up at the moon and smiled, "Happy Birthday, Kayah."

Part Two:

Answers

"Dream deep, because when you do, you will begin to find your answers."
— Michael Bassey Johnson , The Oneironaut's Diary

Chapter 10

When Kayah regained control over her actions, she led the pack back to the clubhouse and shifted. She was too busy trying to find her bag to notice every wolf was on their knees, showing her respect as an Alpha. Finally, Colby walked to her and Demon, "Demon, Kayah, when you are wed, I will renounce my title as Alpha, and you will take my place."

Demon nodded, "When the time is right, I will accept the title of Alpha of this pack."

Kayah nodded, "When the time is right, I will accept the title of Alpha and join my pack with yours."

Colby stood, picked up his clothes, and walked off to the clubhouse with the rest of the pack following him. Kayah and Demon were the last to enter the clubhouse; the sight she saw brought tears to her eyes. While the pack was out running, the mothers of the nursing pups stayed behind and turned the clubhouse into a birthday wonderland.

Demon leaned down and whispered in her ear, "Happy birthday, my love; welcome home."

Kayah turned and looked at the wolf she had loved for years, "You did this?"

"Mom and dad helped. " We wanted to make this special because your parents could not," he said, softly kissing her.

"This means the world to me, Demon; thank you."

"Baby, I will always try and give you the world."

Chloe popped the invisible bubble that surrounded Kayah and Demon, "Kayah, come here."

Smiling, Demon grabbed Kayah's hand and pulled her to the front of the room, where Chloe, Colby, Dezra, Shilo, and Taria waited. They stood behind a table with a mammoth size cake that said Happy Birthday Kayah. She could say nothing due to the knot of emotions caught in her throat.

Seeing the distress on her friend's face,, "So do you want

cake first or open your presents?" asked Dezra.

"I say she opens her presents first," said the stranger.

Kayah turned and looked into eyes she had seen before, "How do you always know where to find me?"

Demon stepped before Kayah, "Hey, that asshole was leaning up against my truck the other day."

The sound in Demon's voice quickly broke through to Shilo, and he joined him, blocking Kayah from the stranger. "Who are you?" asked Shilo.

Kayah pushed Demon to the side so she could get past him and walked up to the stranger saying, "It's okay. He is not here to hurt me."

"Kayah, you know him?" asked Demon.

"I don't know him, but I know of him. This is Onyx, my brother that went missing as a child."

Onyx turned his head and nodded, "Hello, Colby."

Colby was shaken, causing him to stagger, "How is this possible? We looked everywhere for you. Where have you been?"

"That is a story for another time. Tonight is a night of celebration. It is my baby sister's birthday, and I have a gift for you," he said, holding out a small box.

Kayah reached out and took the box. First, she looked at Colby and Demon; when she got the nod of approval, she opened it and pulled out a small ring of keys. "What are these for?" she asked.

"I have been following you since the night our parents were killed. I know Colby gave you our father's leather, and now you have his bike to match. Little sister, if you are going to be the Alpha of two wolf packs, you will also gain our father's MC. Are you sure you are ready for that responsibility?" he asked.

"Onyx, my childhood was taken from me just like it was taken from you. So my question is... If you were always meant to be Alpha, why are you letting me take your place?" Kayah asked.

Onyx looked at his sister and tipped his head to the side,

wondering how much he could tell her with all the others in the room with supersonic hearing. "Little sister, me being in line to be Alpha died long ago. It was taken from me when I disappeared. I am no longer even a member of the pack. That was ripped away from me as well. I am the one that is destined to be a lone wolf for all eternity."

"No matter who you are, Onyx, you deserve to be a part of a pack," Demon said.

"I wish that were true," Onyx said sadly.

"Enough of this sadness; there will be plenty of time for you and Kayah to talk. Tonight is a celebration," Chloe said, hugging Onyx.

Onyx smiled warmly at Chloe and said, " Yes, I want some of that cake. But, of course, knowing my sister, that is a brownie or the biggest decorated cheesecake I have ever seen."

"How do you know?" Kayah asked, lifting her brow.

Onyx laughed and slung an arm around her shoulders, "Because the only thing you like about cake is the frosting."

The night was filled with laughter, congratulations, and wedding plans. Kayah was sitting with Dezra when Demon whispered, "I'll be right back." Kayah watched him walk off and talk with Colby. Demon would look back at her every few minutes and nod to whatever Colby was discussing.

Dezra leaned over and whispered, " I believe he is the sexiest wolf here."

Kayah looked at Dezra with a look of confusion, "Huh? Who?"

"Girl... Oynx."

"He has been back in my life not even an hour, and you are already trying to dig your teeth in," Kayah laughed.

"Look... all I said was that he is sexy. But, he still has me uneasy."

"Dezra, he is my brother. So I think it is safe to say he is safe."

"Something doesn't smell right about him."

"Please don't be looking for places to poke holes and find problems," Kayah pleaded.

"When you ascended, you must have lost your sense of smell. He doesn't smell like a wolf," Dezra said carefully.

Kayah's eyes were trained on her brother as he crossed the room and stood with Colby and Demon. Something in Demon's eyes gave her an uneasy feeling.

∞∞∞∞

Later that evening, Kayah and Demon were lying quietly in the dark when he asked, "Do you think the nightmares will stop now?"

"No clue... one can hope so. What were you, Colby, and Onyx talking about?"

"We were talking about the Timberwolves and the Hunters. Colby has set the pack meeting with Timberwolves for tomorrow night. But Onyx and Colby think that the Hunters are starting to sniff around because of the movement of the Timberwolves," Demon answered.

"Why would they catch on now? Colby did an excellent job

making it look like I was dead, or at least missing."

"That's the problem. The Alpha of the Hunters knew my father and yours were good friends. But, unfortunately, your father's pack went dormant when he was killed. So now that the Timberwolves are headed down here for a pack meeting, Onyx thinks the Hunters are noticing them. I hope we can get the pack here, and they recognize you as their Alpha before we have trouble."

Kayah turned onto her side to see Demon in the moonlit room. She touched his face and smiled; she loved his eyes and how they shimmered in the moonlight. "Demon, do you think I am strong enough to be the Alpha of a pack?"

Demon nodded and kissed her on the forehead, knowing they would not stop there if he touched his lips with hers. Reaching over, he pulled her close, closing the distance between them, and snuggled her tight, hoping the nightmare would stay away for tonight.

As Kayah lay in the dark with Demon, she fought to shut

down the thoughts running through her head. Demon could tell she was still restless, so he started growling low, deep in his chest, to where it sounded like a soft purr. Kayah laid her head on his chest so she could feel the rumbling of his chest; slowly, her mind turned off, and she drifted off to a sound sleep for the first time with no nightmares.

Kayah woke to the shades pulled, and Demon's side of the bed had gone cold. She almost thought last night was a dream until she heard the shower. Then, wanting coffee, she climbed out of bed and padded to the kitchen to find Dezra drinking a coke and eating sausage and a mango.

"How can you drink that sugary shit first thing in the morning?" she mumbled.

"I don't know how you drink that nasty shit you drink either," she retorted.

"What time is it?"

"Almost six am. You must have been worn out; you didn't run last night."

"Last night was the first night I slept with no nightmares. I don't know if it was because of my ascending or Demon. When I fell asleep, I was out; if I dreamed, I don't remember," shrugged Kayah.

"So, what are the plans for today?" Dezra asked.

"Well, I need to figure out what I will say tonight at the pack meeting. I know by pack law I need at least ten members to show. Then over half of them must accept me as their Alpha. Plus hope that all of this goes off without a hitch and without the Hunters showing up."

Not knowing what she could say to help her friend, she ate the rest of her breakfast silently.

Chapter 11

Kayah spent the morning sitting on her deck watching Demon fiddle with his truck and work around the yard. Then, she closed her eyes and opened herself to the world around her. With her new abilities, she could sense Onyx lurking in the woods; she opened her eyes and looked in the direction, she felt him. Kayah could barely see him through the trees. Lifting her hand, she waved.

Onyx was torn between staying hidden in the trees or spending time with his sister. A war of emotions raged within him when she waved. He wanted to spend time with Kayah and her mate... but how would he explain where he has been all his life and the beast he has become. Finally, the longing to know his sister won, and Onyx stepped out of the shadows into the morning sunlight.

Kayah smiled as Onyx climbed the stairs to the deck and patted the chair beside her offering him to sit. Onyx sat and studied his beautiful sister's face; she closely resembled their mother.

"You know you look a lot like our mother," he said quietly.

"Really?" she said with a smile.

He just nodded.

"Can you tell me about her? I know you didn't spend much time with her, but I want to learn anything about our parents."

"I remember she was beautiful, loving, and she loved being a mom. She would have me help. Family was important to our mother; she loved the pack but loved her family more. Mother was sweet and obedient to whatever father said unless it messed with her children, then she was a force to be reckoned with. Our father was an amazing man, and the pack loved him. They were loyal enough to follow him into the seventh circle of hell without asking questions. There are still pack members that mourn his death," Onyx said sadly.

"Brother, that is some big shoes to fill. I don't think I can do it. What happens if I fail? I have lived my life as a lone wolf. How will I lead a pack when I don't know what it is like to belong to one?" asked Kayah.

"I do not doubt that you will fill his shoes just fine. You are an Alpha from the ancient bloodline. Leading is in your blood, plus Demon will be by your side. You are not alone anymore. You will have two packs to back you up."

"You said I have Demon, but what about you?" she asked.

"I will always be by your side. I will never be a part of a pack."

"Why?"

"Because, Kayah, of my past. Things happened a long time ago when I was taken that stopped me from being accepted in to any pack."

"What happened to you?"

"That is something I will not get into right now. But I will tell you when the time is right."

Kayah never liked being told no, but she felt she would push her brother away if she pushed any further. So, she just nodded and stared into the woods.

∞∞∞

As Kayah dressed for the pack meeting, she smiled and thought about the beautiful day she had spent with Onyx. Kayah checked her phone for the hundredth time to see if Dezra had messaged her back, only to find it still message-free. So she stuffed her phone in the back pocket of her jeans, grabbed her father's leather off the bed, and searched for Demon.

She found Demon sitting on the deck, watching the sun disappear behind the treetops. "I'm ready if you are."

Demon stood, grabbed her by the throat, and kissed her hot and demanding. When he broke the kiss, he growled, "I can't wait until you are fully mine." When Demon released his hold on her, she swayed a little while panting. He gave her one last look that made the delta between her legs throb, and then he jogged down the stairs to his truck. Kayah took a couple of deep breaths to stop her body from shaking from the carnal lust she felt.

After climbing in the truck, she glanced at Demon and saw the self-satisfied smirk. "Let's go, smart ass," Kayah said, crossing her arms and looking out the window. Demon snorted and backed down the driveway.

When they pulled into the clubhouse parking lot, she was rendered speechless.

"Looks like Dad successfully got the word out to the Timberwolves."

"Demon, this can't be my father's pack. There are over five hundred bikes here."

"Baby, this is both packs. Over two hundred are Timberwolves, and they are here to see you. So tonight, you will claim your pack; the Timberwolves will now know you are alive."

"Yeah, now the Hunters will know I am alive and start

trouble."

"Go claim your pack, and you will have an army to protect you."

"I don't know if I can do this, Demon... I am scared."

"Baby, look at me." When Kayah looked into his eyes, she could feel his strength. "I will be with you every step of the way. Remember, you are not alone anymore. Plus, to be completely honest, you can do this without me. You are strong, loyal, and brave; they will love you. Come on; the meeting is going to start soon. Go claim your pack."

As Kayah made her way to the front of the room, she heard the whispers.

"Who is that?"

"That wolf almost looks like Nyko."

"What makes this wolf so special...why did we come down here?"

With each step she took, she found her strength. Kayah stood before the group next to Colby and Demon and waited for Colby to call the meeting to order.

Colby: *"Baton Rouge Timberwolves and New Orleans Dire Wolves. I call this meeting to order. Timberwolves, seventeen years ago, your Alpha was murdered along with his mate. You have been without an Alpha, your club without a president for years; that ends tonight. I made it known the night that Nyko died that his daughter Kayah was missing as well. Nyko and I decided if anything were to happen to him, I would raise Kayah and keep her hidden from the world until it was time for her to take her place as your Alpha. Tonight is that night! Kayah, step forward and claim your birthright."*

Kayah: *"I am Kayah daughter of Nyko. I am the true Alpha of this pack. If anyone accepts me as your Alpha, I would like you to show your obedience; please bow."*

Almost every Timberwolf in the clubhouse dropped to their knees and bowed their head.

"How do we know you are truly Kayah? If you want us to follow you and call you our Alpha prove you are the daughter of Nyko," yelled a stranger.

Kayah slipped her arms into her father's leather and pulled it on without hesitation. When she looked into the group, her eyes were glowing a brilliant blue, and she growled, "Now obey and bow before your Alpha."

The last remaining wolves dropped to their knees and lowered their heads.

Kayah: *"Baton Rouge Timberwolves, do you accept me as your only Alpha?"*

All Timberwolves: *"Yes, Alpha!"*

Kayah: *"Stand! Now we will take care of the pack business. First, we will be combining these two wolf packs. Does anyone have a problem with this?"*

All: *"No, Alpha!"*

Kayah: *"Next, I am from the ancient bloodline of wolves that come from Aadya. It is said that I can pass on some of my powers* *to any wolf who attends the wedding and merging of the packs. The wedding will take place on the next full moon. If you think you will show up just to gain the powers… get that out of your head right now. If you receive some of my powers and betray the pack or me, your abilities will be stripped. Because we are combining both packs, you will have two Alphas. Demon is my mate and the next in line to be Alpha of the Dire Wolves. Are all in agreement?"*

All wolves: *"Yes! Alpha."*

Kayah: *"Then I will close this meeting. Feel free to stay and take part in food and drink. Get to know your soon-to-be new pack members."*

For the next couple of hours, Kayah talked with different wolves hearing stories about her parents and how noble her father was. Then, she pulled her phone out of her back pocket and checked it; again, there was no text from Dezra. Kayah looked around the room for Demon, and when he looked at her, she waved him over to her.

"What's up, Babe?"

"Have you seen Dezra tonight?"

"No... But there are a lot of wolves here."

"Demon, I am worried. I texted her and called her. It is not like her not to answer."

"When was the last time you talked to her?"

"This morning, when she left. Dezra told me she was going home to do some laundry and call her mom. If she didn't talk to me later, she would see me tonight at the meeting."

"Okay, don't panic. We will ask around to see if anyone has seen her. If she is not here, then we will stop by her place on the way home."

Dezra was nowhere to be seen. They asked everyone, and no one had seen her. When they told Colby that Dezra had not answered her phone and didn't attend the meeting, he took over and let Kayah and Demon leave. Kayah watched the shadows as Demon drove. The closer they got to Dezra, she tried to sense the presence of her friend, but she came up empty. When they pulled into the driveway, she only relaxed slightly when they saw her car. Before Demon could stop the truck, Kayah opened the door and jumped out, and ran for the door as soon as her feet touched the ground. When she knocked on the door, it creaked open. She pushed open the door and stepped into a nightmare. Dezra's house had been ransacked. Kayah felt genuine fear when she sniffed the air and smelled blood. Not waiting for Demon, Kayah went searching for Dezra. Kayah found Dezra bloody and bound in the bedroom; acting on instinct, Kayah ran to her best friend to help. Kayah dropped to her knees and shook Dezra, relieved to find out she was still alive. That was the last thing Kayah saw before everything went black.

Chapter 12

Demon came to on the hard ground from being shaken by Onyx. His head ached, he touched where it was hurt and felt a good size goose egg, and his hair was wet. Then, pulling back his hand, he saw it was covered in blood. Demon looked up at Onyx just as he caught the scent of blood and watched as fangs grew where Onyx's K-9s were normally, and his eyes went black.

"Holy Fuck! What are you?"

Onyx closed his eyes to gain control over the blood lust; when he opened them, his eyes were back to their usual color.

"Now is not the time to worry about that. Where is Kayah?"

"She's not in the house?"

"No! What happened? The house has been tossed, and the scent of both girls still lingers in the air."

"When Kayah couldn't reach Dezra, we drove out here. She jumped out of the truck and ran into the house before I could stop. After I stopped the truck, I jumped out and ran after her. I took about three steps and lights out; someone or something hit me from behind. Next thing I know, I wake up from you shaking me and a big ass bump on my head."

"Fuck!!! I will put money down that the Hunters have the girls. Please tell me that you two jumped the broom and created the Par bond between you," Onyx snarled.

"No. Kayah and I wanted to keep to the laws. We didn't want to screw up her becoming an Alpha. Can't you feel her?" Demon huffed.

"No, she is too far away. Is Dezra mated to someone?"

"No," Demon answered.

"Fuck!" Onyx yelled while pulling out his phone. "Colby, we have a problem. Demon and Kayah were jumped. Kayah and Dezra are missing. Bring a search party. Demon and I are at Dezra's house." He shoved his phone back in his pocket and looked back at Demon, "Your father is on the way."

"How could I let this happen? How the fuck am I going to be her mate if the first time I needed to protect her and she gets taken," spat Demon.

"It could have happened to anyone of us. They waited until you were distracted and concentrating on her so that they could sneak up on you without detection. I would guess they have been planning this for a while. They took Dezra as bait, so Kayah would be worried about her friend and not pay attention to her surroundings. We will find them. All I need to do is get close enough, and our bond will kick in," Onyx explained.

"How? You two barely know each other. How do you already have a bond?"

"It is a sibling bond from the ancient bloodline. From the minute we shift for the first time, we can sense each other. Then when we ascend, the bond gets stronger."

Before Demon could ask more questions, he focused on the

rumbling of bikes closing in. They watched as hundreds of bikes took up the road, with Colby leading the pack. Colby and Sid walked side by side and joined Demon and Onyx. Colby pulled his son into his arms and said, "We will find her."

Onyx and Sid exchanged nods, "Colby, I believe the Hunters have the girls. It is going to take an army to find them," stated Onyx.

"We are an army. I know she is your sister, but I raised her, and she will marry my son. So Kayah is my daughter, and I will find her. Where do you think they would take the girls?"

"They are from Lafayette…but I don't think they would be stupid enough to take them there. Demon and I can head that way. You can run the search group here and in Baton Rouge. Then if we come up with nothing, we can expand our search."

"That sound like a plan; make sure everyone is in pairs. No one searches alone. We don't need to add fatalities; we must focus on finding the girls," said Demon.

Colby and Sid decided they would talk to the packs, Colby

would run the search for New Orleans, and Sid would overlook the search in Baton Rouge.

"I need to grab some stuff, and then I will be ready to go," Onyx said, walking over to his bike.

Demon watched as he grabbed two 9mm Glocks and four clips from his saddlebags. Walking back, he asked, "Do you know how to use one of these?"

Demon reached around to the small of his back and pulled out his 9mm Glock. "Yes, it is safe to say I know how to use one."

"Do you have enough ammo?"

"I have two extra clips in the glove box."

Onyx nodded and opened the door of Demon's truck, "Let's get moving…time is wasting away."

Demon and Onyx decided to take Hwy 90 because one of the other search groups would be taking US 10. This way, Onyx would sense if they hid the girls in the swamps. They were on the road about ten minutes before Demon started asking Onyx questions.

"Okay, dude, you are going to be my brother. So what the hell are you?"

"I am a wolf...."

"You are more than a wolf."

"Fine...I will tell you under one condition. You tell no one what you learn today. Including Kayah, and I will tell her when the time is right."

"Sure."

"I am what you would call a Hybrid."

"No fucking way. How is that possible?"

"I was kidnapped when I was little. The woman that took me was not human or wolf. She was a vampire. As crazy as it sounds, it is true. She held me captive until I shifted for the first time and then turned me. Because of my bloodline, the transformation mutated, and I became a Hybrid. To survive, I need food and blood. When she turned me, she stole my right to be a part of a wolf pack. She stole my birthright. My father always said he wanted two children, one to be Alpha to the pack and one to run the MC. Because of Cerilla, I lost my life."

"Your sister is going to flip when she finds out."

"She is not to find out," Onyx snarled.

"Why don't you want her to know?"

"She just started to get to know me. I want her to know me before she finds out I am a monster."

"You don't need to worry about that with Kayah. She has been obsessed with vampires her whole life. She loves them."

"Really?"

"Yes. Trust me... It will only make her love you more. So... What ever happened to Cerilla?"

"She is out there searching for me. When I was of age, I ran. With me being part wolf, it makes it easy for me to hide from her. Can we get off this conversation now?"

"Sure. Hey, man, thanks for telling me. We are family. You can trust me. Knowing your sister, you will have a spot in our pack."

Onyx looked out the window shielding the blood tear that slid down his cheek. Then, just as he started to get lost in his thoughts, he felt her.

"Demon, how far from Lafayette are we?" Onyx asked.

"About twenty minutes. Why?"

"Because I can feel her. I don't think she is in Lafayette. I think she is in the outskirts. So keep driving, and I will tell you when we are close."

$$\infty\infty\infty$$

To Demon, it felt like they had been driving for hours. The sun was starting to rise when they narrowed down that the girls were being held in an old factory at the end of Nelson M road. They knew if they tried to rescue the girls in the daylight, was a suicide mission. While they waited for dark, Onyx taught Demon how to mask his presence to others. After they ate, they tried to get some sleep, but that was a lost cause. Demon called Colby and gave him an update, and they decided to keep the pack searching in case of Hunter lookouts reporting back to the Alpha.

Demon and Onyx were dressed for their mission when the crescent moon shone brightly. They moved in the shadows like whispers in the wind; Demon relied on Onyx to lead the way. Demon could see in the dark, but with Onyx's bloodline, he could see perfectly. Demon watched Onyx move inhumanly to sneak up on two guards and snap their necks. They quickly dragged the bodies into the tall weeds then they slipped into the building. After they were in the building, Demon sniffed and caught the scent of Kayah and Dezra. Demon and Onyx found it more challenging to maneuver in the old factory than outside. The factory was bathed in light, and shadows could hardly be seen.

When they finally reached the room where the girls were being held, anger bubbled in Demon and Onyx; both girls were beaten and unconscious. Demon knelt by Kayah and quickly untied her; he lifted her into his arms and waited for Onyx to free Dezra. They carried both girls through the factory and back to the truck. When Demon was back on the road headed back to New Orleans, he noticed that he had a tail.

"Onyx, we have a shadow."

"Yeah, I noticed it about three miles ago."

"What do you suggest we do?"

"How fast will this truck go?"

"Fast enough," Demon said while punching the gas.

The Hunters were hot on their tail and keeping pace. After ten miles, three more trucks joined the chase, trying to box them in. When their plans failed, the Hunters started tapping Demon's truck making him swerve and squeal his tires. When they crossed into swam territory, the Hunter gave one last nudge to the tail end of Demon's truck, making him lose control and tip the truck on its side, sliding two hundred feet down the road.

Onyx could no longer contain his anger and let the monster he was loose. Demon watched as his soon-to-be brother went from an overprotective wolf to a true predator of the night.

Onyx sank his fangs into the first Hunter and tasted human/ wolf blood in years. Then the blood touched his tongue; the blood lust was too strong to control. So he went from man to man, ripping them to shreds and creating an ocean of blood and body parts on the highway. Demon was in a trance, watching the massacre in front of him. When shots were fired, and Onyx took three bullets to the chest, it broke his trance, making him react. Demon gripped the 9mm, took aim, and emptied the clip into two shooters while Onyx took care of the last one. Onyx collapsed on the ground next to the truck when the bloodbath was done.

Demon climbed out of the truck's window and knelt beside Onyx, "Dude if you are immortal, why are you not healing?"

"I need blood for my body to heal. I can heal without it. It will just take a lot longer."

Demon held out his wrist, "Drink."

"No...I told myself a long time ago I would never feed on

human/wolf blood again. I don't trust myself to stop."

"I trust you. I need your help. Kayah and Dezra need your help. Now drink, god dammit, and heal yourself. I know I have a couple of broken ribs from the truck flipping. The girls were already in bad shape before the accident. They need to get to a hospital."

Onyx grabbed Demon's wrist and sank his fangs in. Demon watched as Onyx drank; his body pushed out the bullets, and the wounds closed. Keeping Kayah in his mind helped Onyx stop draining Demon of blood. Onyx and Demon carefully pulled the girls out of the mangled truck and carried them as far as possible. Demon called Colby and told him what had happened. It wasn't long before they heard the rumble of bikes. Demon almost wept with relief when he saw his mom driving the SUV. They loaded the girls in the back and told her to take them straight to the hospital, and they would meet them there.

Demon and Onyx went with the pack and cleaned themselves up before heading to the hospital to stop any unwanted questions. The people of New Orleans had heard rumors of people that could turn into wolves, and there was no reason to make the stories true. When Demon finally reached the hospital, the sight that greeted him shattered his heart. He stood in the doorway of Kayah's room and felt helpless seeing the love of his life on life-support.

Chapter 13

Demon felt his reality was spinning out of control; he slowly walked over to the chair next to the bed and sank into the seat. He gripped Kaya's hand softly as if she was a china doll that would break. Demon sat for hours in silence, listening to the beeps and hum of the machines pumping life into her. His mother's voice broke the silence, and the barrier kept his tears from falling.

"Son, has the Dr talked to you yet?" she asked.

Saying nothing, Demon just shook his head.

"I have been going between both rooms."

Demon's voice cracked when he spoke, "How is Dezra?"

"She is in bad shape, Demon. The Dr said that both the girls have head trauma. Kayah's left hip and shoulder are broken, and four broken ribs. Dezra's brain was bleeding; they had to remove part of her skull to help with the swelling. Her right leg is shattered. She also had internal bleeding, but they were able to stop that. They don't know when or even if Dezra will ever wake."

Demon hung his head and let his tears stream down his dark chocolate cheeks. It didn't take long for his sorrow to turn into white-hot rage.

"Get a hold of my father. I want him here, and have you seen Onyx?"

"Demon, what are you planning?"

"Answer the questions," he growled.

"Demon, I know you are scared...but you will not talk to me in that tone. I don't care if you are going to be Alpha. I am still your mother. You will treat me with respect. Do you understand, boy?" Chloe barked.

"I'm sorry, Mom. I need to get things in order before the Hunters find out where the girls are at. I don't need them to come and finish what they started. I need you to call Dad. I need to know where Onyx is and see if he is okay. I need to make a plan to keep Kayah and Dezra safe while they heal. Could you do this so I can stay here and protect them? I wonder if we can get Dezra moved in here, that way we only have one room to guard, plus it will help the girls heal faster knowing they are together."

"That's all you had to say. I will call your father; the last I knew, Onyx was with him. I will also arrange to have Dezra moved in here with Kayah."

Demon nodded his thanks and turned back to Kayah. He lifted her battered hand to his lips and kissed it gently.

$$\infty \infty \infty$$

For the next couple of weeks, Demon watched Drs and nurses come and go out of the room to check on Kayah and Dezra. They had decided to keep two guards outside of the room at all times, and every couple of hours, someone would come and relieve him so he could eat, shower, and try and sleep. Kayah and Dezra were treated like royalty by the hospital staff, and it seemed every day, more flowers would appear from the staff and friends they worked with.

On week three, the doctor removed the breathing tube and took Kayah off life support because she was now breathing independently. However, from the brain scans and tests they have been running daily, they still had no idea when or if they would ever wake from the coma. So by the middle of the third week, the nurses had maintenance pull in a cot next to Kayah's bed so Demon could sleep.

Week six Demon heard a weak voice asking for water, "Water, please."

Demon looked at Kayah and watched her eyes flutter a couple of times, and then they opened to show her beautiful blue eyes. He gently cupped her cheeks and kissed her lips softly, making her lips curl in a small smile.

"Water...Demon, please," she croaked.

Demon quickly poured her a glass of water with a straw and

lowered it for her to take a drink. Unfortunately, when the cold water hit her dry throat, it made her cough.

"Drink slowly, Kai," Demon gently scolded.

"Oh, I hurt all over. I feel like I was hit by a train. Where is Dezra? Is she okay?"

"Shhhh, Baby, you just woke up. There will be time for answers. Dezra is in the bed next to you. She hasn't woken up yet. You hurt because you have quite a few broken bones," Demon explained, pushing the button for the nurse.

Kayah broke when she saw Dezra fighting for her life in the bed beside her. Demon slid into bed next to Kayah and held her as she cried. When murmuring didn't help calm her, he started the low Alpha purr and shifted to where her head lay on his chest. When the tremors from crying left her body, he was sure Kayah was sleeping once again.

When Kayah woke for the second time, she looked up at Demon. He looked into her sad eyes and asked, "Do you want anything to eat?"

Kayah shook her head, nuzzled back into his chest, and fell asleep. This was her routine for the next couple of days. When Demon could get her to eat, she only ate in small doses. Kayah seemed to perk up when Dezra was healed enough to come off life supports then she returned to her new routine of silence. When the pack members would visit, she would barely talk. Demon knew if Dezra died, Kayah would fade away completely.

The following week, the doctor cleared Kayah to finish her recovery at home. When it was time to leave, Kayah lay lifeless in the bed staring out the window, ignoring everything Demon or the nurse said. Demon shook his head and bent down to pick her up, and she sprang to life.

Kayah screamed and raged, fighting everyone with every bit of strength. "NO! I will not leave her here broken and alone."

When she heard her brother's voice, she stopped fighting. "Kayah, stop fighting the people trying to help you. You need to go home and finish healing. Staying here is not helping Dezra."

Kayah covered her face and wept, knowing he was right. She

looked at Onyx with tear-stained cheeks, "If I leave, she will be alone. She is in this mess because of me. They took her, knowing I would come after her. This was all my fault. She will never forgive me if I am not here when she wakes."

Onyx walked over to the bed and sat beside Kayah's hip, "Sis, listen to me; none of this is your fault. The bastards started this war when they killed our parents."

"They killed our parents because of me. I was there that night, and I remember everything. They gang-raped and tortured our mother before killing her, then executed our father because they protected me. Are you sure you want to be around me? All I do is bring death to the people I love."

"Stop it, Kayah! You are feeling sorry for yourself. If you want to be pissed off about what happened, then be pissed off. Stop blaming yourself for things that are out of your control. You are one of the Alphas of a wolf pack, so stop the pity party and act like one. Dezra may be your best friend, but you are still her Alpha," Demon growled.

"Demon is right. Stop feeling sorry for yourself and get your ass out of that bed. It would be best to focus on returning to your full strength. But what happens if you are still in this pity party and they attack? Your pack is left defenseless, and that would be your fault. So what are you going to do? " Will you keep blaming yourself, or will you do what you need to do?" asked Onyx.

"What do I do about Dezra? She will be alone."

"I will stay here with her," said Onyx.

"You will call me as soon as she wakes?"

"Yes, Sis, I will. Now go with your man and get better."

Kayah looked at Dezra one last time, then swung her legs over the edge of the bed and stood for the first time.

∞∞∞

After Kayah said her goodbyes and whispered to Dezra that she would return as soon as she woke up, she left the hospital with Demon. While in the parking lot, she noticed that Demon was driving his mother's SUV and looked at him questionably.

"My truck was totaled in the accident when Onyx and I rescued you and Dezra," he said, opening the door for her.

Demon lifted Kayah into the seat and shut the door. Then, after they were on the road, he finally asked the million-dollar question, "Kai, what happened after you were taken?"

"Well...I found Dezra unconscious, bleeding, and tied up on the floor. When I knelt to untie her, I was hit on the head. I woke up in a locked room with Dezra shaking me. When the door opened, my nightmare walked through the door. One of the men that killed my parents was our captor. His orders were to take us to the Alpha when he returned from the run he was on. So when he returned to bring us some food, we tried to escape. Dezra and I got lost in the big factory, and when they caught up with us, we fought as hard as possible. Dezra fell and hit her head on the corner of a giant concrete pillar. I thought she was dead. I killed three of them before they overpowered me. The only satisfaction was I ripped out the throat of one of the men that killed my parents. I remember them breaking one of our legs so that we couldn't escape anymore, and they kept us drugged. The next thing I know, I am waking up in the hospital with you holding my hand and feeling like I got hit by a bus. Now explain what happened to your truck."

"I was knocked out when you were taken, and I woke by Onyx shaking me. When we realized the Hunters had taken you, he called my father and set up search parties. Onyx and I decided to head to Lafayette up Hwy 90. He found you by your sibling bond. We waited until nightfall to enter the factory, found you both, and left just as quickly. We thought we were in the home stretch until we saw we had a tail. It turned into a highway speed chase. Four trucks were trying to box us in, and when that wouldn't work, they bumped my truck and flipped it on its side. Onyx and I killed the men chasing us, and we called for help. The pack showed up with my mom driving the SUV, and she took you and Dezra to the hospital. You know the rest."

"So what do we do from here? How do we stop this from

happening again?" she asked.

"Well, the first thing we should do is call a pack meeting so they all can see that they can see their Alpha is up and ready to fight."

"Then that's what we will do," Kayah said with determination.

Chapter 14

Over the next few weeks, Kayah and Demon focused on her rehab and pulling the pack into a tighter group. Kayah was fixing her and Demon's lunch when her phone started ringing; without looking, she answered.

"She-Bitch!" Dezra croaked. "I feel like a train wreck."

Hearing Dezra's voice made her cry with relief. "Dezra, how many times have I told you not to call me that?" she sniffled.

"Come get me out of here. You know how much I hate being the patient."

"I am on my way."

As Kayah got to the car, she yelled for Demon, "Come on, we got to go."

Demon jogged down the deck stairs, following her, "Where's the fire? Where are we going?"

"Dezra is awake; come on, let's go," Kayah said, slamming the SUV door.

A smile bloomed on Demon's face as he opened the driver's door. The drive to the hospital felt like it was taking forever, making Kayah antsy. So history would not repeat itself; Demon pulled up to the hospital doors and let Kayah out. Kayah took the stairs two at a time because waiting for the elevator would take precious time. When she reached the fifth floor, she ran to the room, skidding to a stop. When entering the room, she smiled, seeing Dezra sitting up, eating her beloved Conecuh sausage and mangos, and drinking a coke.

"Now, how and the hell did you get that? This hospital does not serve that for meals here."

"Dude, she would not shut up about it. So I went and got it for her. But, please, for the love of god, let her eat it. This is the first she has been quiet," Onyx said with a smirk.

Kayah climbed into bed with Dezra and enjoyed watching her lifelong friend shovel in food. A little time later, Demon walked in and chuckled at the sight. Then, he pulled up a chair next to Onyx. They talked quietly while the girls caught up on the last two and a half months they were apart. Kayah filled in the blanks and what happened while Dezra finished eating.

"So you are telling me that Onyx and Demon rescued us?"

"Yes."

"Holy hell…How long was I out?" Dezra asked.

"Two and a half months."

"Fuck! I missed your wedding. I am so sorry, Kayah."

"You missed nothing. Do you think I could get married without you? Plus, there will be some changes, and I don't care if you don't like them. But, as your Alpha, you will obey them," Kayah said, crossing her arms and waiting for a fight.

"What are these changes?" asked Dezra.

"You will be moving in with Demon and me until the Hunters are taken care of. Onyx will be staying there too. Your house is not safe to stay at. It will be safer if we stay in a group."

"If I agree, you must promise me something too."

"What is that?"

"That means no more late-night runs for you."

"I agree," said Kayah, shocking Dezra into silence. "Now, let's see what it will take to bust you out of here."

"That is the best thing I have heard all day," Dezra said, rubbing her hands together.

"I will go find out," Demon said while standing.

It took about three hours to get Dezra discharged from the hospital. On the way home, they stopped at Dezra's house to pick up some of her stuff and then headed home.

∞∞∞

Kayah and Dezra worked on wedding plans, while Demon and Onyx worked on finding out what the Hunters' next move was. Demon and Onyx stayed close to the girls ensuring their safety because they still were not at full strength.

"Girl, your wedding is in two days. Are you ready to be a wife and Alpha of a huge wolf pack?"

"Yes. I fall in love with Demon a little more every day. I am ready for our souls to become one."

"I am happy for you. I hope I can find that in a mate someday. But, unfortunately, I don't think that will be in the cards for me."

"You will find someone; I know you will. Dezra, you are a wonderful person with a lot of love to give," smiled Kayah. Then, she looked down at the little bags of rice, and her smile faded, "Dezra, I am so sorry that my past has spilled over into your life."

"What the hell are you talking about?"

"You were hurt because of me...I know it's my fault. They knew if they took you, I would come after you."

"Girl, it's not your fault those fuck-twats are psychos. I am your ride-or-die. You are my family. Do us both a favor and stop blaming yourself. Just because you are now my Alpha, I can and will knock some sense into you."

"I will try. D, I know if I tell you this, you will understand me.

I want to kill every one of them. Not only do I want justice for what they did to us…I want vengeance for my parents. I want to feel their flesh rip from my claws. I want to feel their neck snap and watch as the life drains out of their eyes," Kayah said as her body shook.

"Kayah, are you sure you can live with the aftermath?"

"Yes."

"Then I won't talk you out of it. I will be right there with you."

"You don't need to do that."

"Bitch…Did you forget that I was the one taken? I don't blame you…I blame them. I want to see them dead just as bad as you."

Kayah could only nod as she tied another ribbon around a small pouch of rice. When Dezra was satisfied that Kayah laid the conversation to rest, she continued making Kayah's wedding decorations.

On the evening of the wedding, Onyx reported that the Hunters were quiet and had no word of revenge for the death of their pack members. He hoped that tonight would go off without any problems. He wanted his sister to have at least one happy memory to start her new life. He watched Dezra run around the clubhouse, ensuring every thing was perfect for Kayah and Demon. He felt an electric pull toward the dark chocolate beauty. Her big brown eyes called to a place he thought was dead in him. His fingers itched to touch, and his lips tingled whenever he thought about pushing her up against a wall and kissing her just to shut her up. Yet, every time she smiled, the darkness that overshadowed his life dissipated.

"Hey…Hey…You…Calling the sexy piece of white chocolate," yelled Dezra.

"Are you talking to me?"

"No. I am talking to the tall, mysterious white man behind you. Yes, smart one, I am talking to you. Come over here and help me move these two tables," Dezra huffed, fisting her hands on her hips.

"You know, smart mouth, one of these days you will regret smarting off to me."

"Listen, white boy... I am too much woman for you. You can't handle all this chocolate. I would eat you alive. Now are you going to help me or not?" she laughed.

Onyx pushed off the wall shaking his head. He played moving crew for the next hour as Dezra rearranged the room.

"How many wolves do you think will show up tonight?" asked Dezra.

"If they all have brains...all of them," Colby answered as he entered the room.

"Well, I hope they get here soon. The wedding is only an hour away."

"It is a tradition that no bikes will be here tonight. This is strictly pack business. We are merging both packs tonight so that everyone will be here, that includes adults and children," explained Colby.

After leaving Onyx and Dezra to finish decorating, Colby searched for Kayah. Kayah was sitting outback of the clubhouse watching the sunset; at that moment, she was a perfect image of Asheara.

"Hey, kiddo, are you ready for tonight?"

"Yes and no," she said with a weary look.

"What are you worried about?" asked Colby.

"I am ready to start my new life with Demon by my side. Being Alpha to a wolf pack is scary to me. I was seen as an outcast by the Dire Wolves all my life, and the Timberwolves thought I was dead. So going from having no family to having a huge family is a little scary. I am ready to take my father's place as their Alpha. Just scared I won't live up to his name."

"Kayah, your father was my best friend, and I was proud to call him my brother. I raised you as a promise to him and because I wanted to. I love you as if you were my own. If I could have done it differently, I would have; I am so sorry you grew up as an outcast. After tonight by pack law, you will be my daughter. As I told you, I had always hoped you and Demon would be mated for life; as for being Alpha, your father's blood runs through your veins. Every time we butted heads when you were growing up, the Alpha in you always showed. I will always be here to help guide you if you need help. Just because I am stepping down as Alpha does not mean I will disappear. I know I haven't told you, but Kayah, I am very proud of you and proud to call you my daughter. Chloe and I love you very much,"

Kayah's eyes filled with tears as the last fracture in her heart healed. Kayah looked at Colby as the tears started to fall, "Colby, I have waited all my life to hear you say that."

"Well, sweetheart, it is something I should have always told you. So now let's get you married."

"We don't have to mate in front of everyone, do we?"

"Dear god...No, who and the hell told you that?"

"Some of the older pack members."

"No... the par bond will be created tonight before the pack.

I don't want to know anything about my children's sex life,"

Colby laughed.

Chapter 15

When Onyx and Kayah entered the meeting hall, she noticed over five hundred wolves were there to witness her wedding. She looked over at Demon and saw her future. Candles and the moonlight lit the room. When she looked up, she noticed they had opened the roof to where everyone's eyes glowed in the moonlight. Kayah now knew why she and Demon were required to wear black robes.

Onyx joined her hands with Demon's, and after he kissed her cheek, he took his place next to Dezra. The more he was around her, the harder it was for him to control his primal male instinct for this woman. Onyx badly wanted to make Dezra his, but he knew when she found out that he was a monster, she would never accept him. He still chickened out, telling Kayah who he truly was. But he knew by pack law after tonight;

Demon would no longer be able to keep his secret. They had twenty-four hours after the par bond to tell all their secrets, or the par bond would fail. In the short time Onyx had gotten to know Kayah, he knew she needed to hear it from him, not someone else. Onyx returned to reality when the elbow jabbed him in the side.

"White boy...pay attention. Your sister is getting married and about to be the top Bitch to these wolves."

Saying nothing, he gave Dezra a tiny nod and turned his attention to Colby, bringing the meeting to order.

Colby: *"Wolves...Tonight you will bear witness to the union of these wolves. With their union, we will be merging the two wolf packs. With their union, our packs will be united forever. Is there anyone here that objects to the union of these Alphas?"*
All wolves: *"No, Alpha!"*

Colby: *"Then let's begin. "Chloe, bind their hands with the braided leather unity straps."*

As she bound their hands, Kayah felt their souls interwind

together.

Colby: *"Let this leather binding be your strength in holding you together when times are tough. This binding is for life; only death will release you from this binding. Chloe, it is time for the unity candle."*

Kayah and Demon took the long-handled match from Chloe with their bound hands and lit the candle.

Colby: *"As you light this candle, let its light guide you out of the darkness. May you find this flame in the moon's glow when you run at night. Chloe, give them the goblet."*

After handing Chloe the burned-out match, they took the goblet filled with a red pomegranate wine.

Colby: *"When you drink, remember you are drinking in the eternal love of the gods. Let this wine fuel your love and passion for each other, never letting it dry out. May this wine fill your heart with love for the wolf pack you both shall rule. You now may drink."*

With their bound hands, Demon lifted the goblet to Kayah's

lips and let her take a big gulp; in return, Kayah lifted the goblet to Demon's lips allowing him to drink the rest of the wine. When the wine was gone, Chloe took the goblet and returned to her spot next to Dezra and Onyx.

Colby: *"Now you will exchange your vows to each other for us all to bear witness to and hold you to the laws of the pack. Kayah, you are the Timberwolf pack's Alpha; you will go first."*

Kayah: *"Demon, I am the Timberwolf Alpha; I bring my pack to join with yours not to step down but to rule by your side. As you accept me as your life mate, you will accept my pack as your own. You will show your love for me to the rest of the pack. I will not mate with any other wolf or man in our lifetime. I will stand by your side in good and bad times. I will run by your side under the moon. Demon, you have been there for me my whole life. As others saw me as an outcast, you saw me as family. When the nightmares started when I was sixteen, you ran with me every night. When I told you to leave me alone and that I would never be your mate, you took that as a challenge to make me yours. So I stand in front* *of our packs to vow that I will be your mate for life and make our*

lives one."

Demon: *"Kayah, I will soon be the Alpha of Dire Wolves; I bring*

my pack to join yours, not to step down but to rule by your side. As

you accept me as your life mate, you will accept my pack as your

own. You will show your love for me to the rest of the pack. I will

not mate with any other wolf or woman in our lifetime. I will stand

by your side in good and bad times. I will run by your side under the

moon. Kayah, I fell in love with you when you were sixteen, broken

and alone. The Alpha in you that makes you strong has always

called to me. I knew we were fated from the first meeting, but you

always said we were forbidden. So I stand in front of our packs to

vow that I will be your mate for life and make our lives one."

Colby: *"We will prepare for them to complete the par bond.*

Kayah and Demon shift into your wolf forms."

Kayah and Demon untied the sash and let the robes slide off

their shoulders to pool at their feet. Bones popped and shifted,

and hands and feet became paws. Fur sprouted everywhere,

and their eyes glowed. Kayah was a much bigger wolf than Demon; with her being a Timberwolf, she was naturally taller than him. But with her coming from ancient bloodlines, she towered over him. Kayah looked down at Demon and tipped her head. Then, to show her submission to him and only him, she bent her front legs and lowered her head, giving access to her shoulder. Demon tipped his head back and howled, then sank his canines into Kayah's shoulder, drawing blood and claiming his mate. Kayah cried in ecstasy, feeling the bond start winding its way around her heart. She whimpered softly when Demon licked the bite to stop the bleeding.

Kayah felt butterflies in her stomach when she stood and looked down at Demon once again. She knew they would be together forever once she completed the rest of the ritual. Demon repeated the act of submission to Kayah, and when she howled, she never noticed that every wolf had shifted. The pack started transforming when her canines sank into Demon's shoulder, completing the par bond. As Kayah licked his wound, the wolf pack adjusted to their new abilities. All the wolves now had gained Kayah's speed and healing abilities; silver was their only weakness. Demon stood next to Kayah and looked at their pack. They tipped their heads back and howled, and the pack howled back in return showing their respect.

After everyone returned to their human form and secured their robes, Colby resumed the meeting.

Colby: *"By pack law and the state of Louisiana, I now pronounce you man and wife. Demon, you may now kiss your bride."*

"Fuck, I have been waiting for this minute my whole life," growled Demon.

"Then shut up and kiss me," taunted Kayah.

As quick as lightning, Demon shot out his hand, gripped Kayah's neck, and pulled her to him. With the other hand, he twisted it in her hair at the base of her head and pulled, making her head tip back. Finally, he wrapped it around her back, letting go of her throat and pulling her body flush with his. Then, for the first time, Demon took his kiss instead of giving one. The kiss and the growl weakened Kayah's knees, so she wouldn't slide boneless to the floor Demon tightened his grip, supporting her weight. When Demon released her from the kiss, she was shaky on her legs and saw stars.

"That shut up that smart mouth of yours, didn't it, wife?" Demon smirked.

Kayah was too dazed to devise a smart remark, but she promised he would pay.

Colby: *"There is only one matter left for this meeting. I, Colby, Alpha of the Dire Wolf pack, step down and let my son, Demon take my place. Demon, do you accept this responsibility? Now only will you have your own family to look after you are responsible for the safety and well-being of this pack."*

Demon: *"Yes, I accept this responsibility. I will love and care for every wolf in this pack as I would for my family. From this day forward, this pack will be my family."*

Colby: *"New Orleans Wolves, I give you your new Alphas, Kayah, and Demon."*

The wolf pack cheered and whistled, making them feel welcome.

Demon: *"Kayah and I are now closing this meeting. The rest of the night is to have fun and celebrate. Since there are so many of you, if we don't get to talk to you personally, thank you all for coming and sharing this special night with us. Because of safety reasons for Kayah and Dezra, we will not have the standard pack run under the moon this month. So to be safe, all wolves are banned from running at night. We will cover these issues at our next pack meeting when the children are absent. We have made sure all the beds in the clubhouse have been made up, and parents are welcome to put their sleepy pups to sleep. So please stay and enjoy the food and drink. Kayah and I will let you know when the next pack meeting is. Once again, thank you all for coming. This meeting is now closed. Start the music."*

As the music started, Kayah leaned her shoulder into

Demon, and he placed his arm around the small of her back.

She looked up and said, "Nicely put, babe."

Demon kissed her on her temple, "This is just the beginning, my love."

Chapter 16

During the after-party, Kayah felt like she had danced with every male pack member except her brother; but then she remembered that Onyx was not a member of the pack. So as she danced with Colby, she searched the room for him.

"Have you seen Onyx?" she asked.

"He needed to take care of some personal business; he said he would be gone about an hour. He should be back shortly."

Kayah stopped dancing and studied Colby with a look of concern, "What personal business?"

"That is something you will need to ask him."

The feeling of unease started bubbling in the pit of her stomach, "Colby, where is my brother?"

"Kayah, when wolves take an oath of silence for another, that bond can not be broken. You need to ask Onyx because it is not my secret to tell."

"Why do you know, but I don't?"

"Because when he came back into your life, I needed to make sure he was not a threat to you."

"Colby, he is my brother."

"It didn't matter. He had been missing for years. Then he just popped up on your birthday after you ascended. I needed to make sure."

"Colby, if Onyx wanted to hurt me, he would have done it long ago."

Colby's eyes slanted and went hard, showing the Alpha he truly was, "What the fuck do you mean, Kayah."

"Onyx had stayed in the shadows, watching me since that dreaded night when our parents were killed. Every night I ran under the moonlight, he ran with me without me knowing. I first noticed him a week before my birthday. The night I had dinner at your house and stormed out."

"Are you talking about the night I gave your father's leather to you?"

"Yes, I had a funny feeling, and when I looked into the woods, all I could do was see his eyes. Then the next night, I saw him just inside the woods in wolf form."

"Why am I just now finding this out, Kayah?"

"Because, Colby, growing up for me was not easy. When I was able to live on my own, I started taking care of myself. Remember, I was an outcast to the pack and lived as a lone wolf. Plus, you pissed me off that night. I wasn't ready to tell you. Then my birthday came, and Onyx showed up."

"I am sorry you felt that you couldn't come to me with this. I know that was my fault. I knew keeping you away from the pack was important, but I should have never held you at arm's length from me. That will be the great shame I will carry to my grave. Please know I am always here for you. I know I'm not your father, but I am your father-in-law."

"One of the beautiful things about the future is that it is unwritten. So we have plenty of time to repair what was broken. I will work on putting the past behind me if you work on letting me in. We can fix what was broken if we both work at it."

"I agree. There is one thing I want from this new start."

"What is that?"

"Chloe and I want a pack of grandchildren. I wasn't a good father to you, but I promise to be a terrific papa to those babies."

Kayah tipped her head back and laughed, "I don't know about a pack of children, but I do want kids. How many are you wanting?"

"Oh, eight or nine sounds good."

"How about we start with a couple and go from there?"

When Demon heard Kayah laugh, he looked in her direction, and his heart burst with joy, seeing that she and Colby had started repairing the rift between them.

The blood of a stag still lingered on Onyx's tongue as he stepped back into the clubhouse. He was dreading what he needed to do next, but he knew there was no avoiding it any longer. Onyx scanned the room and spotted Kayah dancing and laughing with Colby. He took in a deep breath and crossed the room. He cleared his throat and asked, "May I cut in and dance with my sister?"

Colby nodded and stepped aside, and Onyx clasped her hand and placed his other hand on the small of her back. As they danced, he wondered if this would be the last time he would spend with his sister once she knew. As they moved to the beat of the music, she itched to pepper him with questions. When the song finished, he looked down at his little sister and softly said, "Can we go somewhere quiet to talk? I need to tell you something, and I am sure I will lose you after you find out the truth."

"Is it why you had to leave for a while tonight?"

"Yes."

"Okay, let's go talk."

"Before we leave, we need to get Demon."

"Demon? Does he know what you are about to tell me?"

"Yes…and before you get upset at him, I made him promise that he would keep my secret. I knew you needed to hear this from me."

Kayah nodded and walked with Onyx to ask Demon to join them.

"Hey brother, I am getting ready to talk to Kayah and relieve you of your promise. That way, you can keep your word to me and strengthen your par bond.

"Where are we headed?" Demon asked as he slung an arm around Kayah's shoulders.

"With both of us with Kayah, a short walk in the woods should be fine. But, I want to make sure that no one else overhears."

"Oh, no…I don't think so…If we go into the woods, you can disappear if you think I don't like what you say. Onyx, you are my brother, and I don't care what you have to say. I love you just the way you are. Nothing you can tell me will make me not want you in my life."

"I won't run or disappear. I need to make sure no one overhears us. I need to explain why I can never be a part of your pack and what happened to me when I was taken as a child."

"As I said, Onyx, I am here to stay. You are my brother, and I love you."

Onyx gave Kayah one last weary look and walked into the woods. They were so wrapped up in what he would tell Kayah they never saw Dezra follow them into the woods. In the middle of the woods was a firepit with benches made from trees for the pack. Dezra watched as Demon and Onyx made a small fire that put off a slight glow that would go undetected. Dezra knew she screwed up when she leaned forward and snapped a twig under her foot.

"Come on out… I know you're there, smart mouth," Onyx said calmly.

Dezra stepped out from behind the tree, "Why are you all out in the woods hiding in the dark?"

"Because I need to talk to Kayah about something, and I don't want anyone else to overhear."

Dezra decided to make herself known that she would stay for this conversation by walking over and sitting next to Kayah. "Well, what's the big news?"

"I like you, Dezra...I like you a lot. So maybe it is good you are here. That way, when you discover what type of monster I am, I will only have to deal with the heartbreak once."

"Brother, I think you will be surprised how they will react," Demon said, placing a hand on his shoulder to show support.

"Okay...I was taken from my family in the middle of the night by a creature, and her name was Cerilla. She kept me captive for years. When I turned sixteen, she turned me into what she was, or at least she tried. But, because of my bloodline, it mutated me into something completely different...

"Onyx, you are a Hybrid. I already knew," Kayah interrupted.

Onyx stared at his sister in amazement. "How did you find out? Who told you?"

"No one told me. First of all, your body temp is too low for a wolf. Second, I couldn't hear your heartbeat when you hugged me until I strained to listen. Third, I was semi-conscious when you and Demon rescued us. Then, sometime after the wreck, I woke up for just a few minutes. I saw you take three bullets to the chest and still live. Then, when my eyes were too heavy to open, I remember Demon telling you to drink his blood," Kayah said, smiling.

"I knew it because Kayah and I talked. I know you are a white boy. But your sexy ass is pale white. So I knew something was different about you the night of Kayah's birthday party. Then when Kayah and I started researching the ancient bloodlines from Aadya, we discovered that many other creatures came from there," Dezra smirked.

"Brother, we may have been born here, but we all came from

Aadya. As I said, you needed to trust your family. I know the heart of wolves, and I know my girl," said Demon.

"I don't know what to say. I know you said she would accept me the way I am... But I didn't want to get my hopes up," Onyx said quietly.

"Why?" Kayah asked.

"Because I am a monster! I have to drink blood to survive."

Kayah stood and approached her brother, "Onyx, you are still a wolf. You are a wolf and then some. Answer me this... Do you feed off humans or other wolves?"

"No... I refuse to drink from wolves and humans because the blood lust becomes too strong. So I feed on animals, mainly deer."

"So that means you are not a threat to the pack or humans. Just because you need blood to survive doesn't mean you are a monster. Wolves need red meat, humans need food, Cows need grass, and frogs need insects. Every living creature needs something to live. So you drink blood and eat red meat. You are still you, and during the next pack meeting, Demon and I will be making you a member of the pack."

"Kayah..."

"She is right, Onyx. You belong with this pack; you are still part Timberwolf."

"That's right white boy...When you are officially a member of this pack, that makes you, by pack law, mine to claim," Dezra said, rubbing her hands together.

Moving quick as lightning, Onyx picked Dezra up and pinned her against the tree. Then, with a wicked look, he crushed his mouth on hers. Dezra went limp from the kiss. So she wouldn't slide to the ground, Onyx placed his knee between her legs catching her weight. When he released her from the kiss, Dezra had nothing witty to say for the first time. So he leaned in and whispered into her ear, "I told you I would shut that smart mouth of yours one day."

Before he released her, Onyx kissed her once again softly, then picked her up, carried her back to her spot on the bench, and sat her down. Then saying loud enough for the others to hear him, "To be technical, by pack law, if the male is an Alpha, they choose their mate. My sister and Demon may be the Alphas of this pack; I have Alpha blood that runs through my veins. So, Dezra, you are mine."

Chapter 17

Onyx carried a shell-shocked Dezra on the walk back to the clubhouse to find the party still going strong. When she heard the music Dezra seemed to come back to reality and wiggled so Onyx would put her down.

"So if you are going to manhandle me and claim I am yours, you are going to dance with me," she said, grabbing his hand and pulling him to the dance floor.

Kayah laughed and snuggled into Demon, "They have no idea what they are in for."

"Why do you say that?"

"Come on, Demon; we have known Dezra for years...we understand what it is like dealing with her. But, on the other hand, Onyx doesn't seem like he is the sit-back and suffer-in-silence type. So they both are going to have their hands full."

"Yeah...but they will be good for each other. When Dezra and Shilo were matched up, I knew it was a bad fit. But, in this crazy world, Onyx and Dezra are a good fit."

"So, are you mad at me for not telling you about Onyx?"

"No. In the haze, I remember him making you promise not to tell me. Are you mad I didn't tell you I knew?"

"No. Baby, he is your brother. I knew you would talk to me when you were ready."

"Today has been a day, and I am exhausted."

"I saw that you and my dad started fixing your rift. It made me happy to see."

"Yeah, we are going to work on it. Do you know he told me he wants grandkids?"

"That doesn't surprise me. Believe it or not, mom and dad love kids."

"Demon, he said he wanted a pack of grandkids...like eight or nine," she said, looking up at him.

"Ummm. What did you say?"

"I told him I wanted children, but I don't think we will have that many."

"I agree…I think five is a good number," he answered, kissing her temple.

"Demon…I told him two, maybe three."

Demon smiled and said, "We will talk about it."

∞∞∞

After the party started to die out and the pack members started to leave, Kayah watched as Dezra handed Onyx the keys to my Jeep and climbed into the passenger side. Demon and Onyx shared a look and continued to get in the vehicles. Kayah knew the look they gave each other was a signal, meaning something didn't smell right, and for them to take opposite ways home.

"Demon, what's going on?" Kayah asked.

"Onyx and I caught the scent of wolves."

"Demon, there were over five hundred wolves here tonight."

"Not those wolves. We caught the scent of wolves from the night we rescued you. We caught the sent of at least two of them. I think they were lookouts to see what we were doing tonight."

"If they saw what happened here tonight, they would be stupid to attack. Our pack has over five hundred members, and I am useless to them now that the par bond is in place—all of the pack members here received new abilities. Are they..."

The ringing of her cell phone cut off Kayah. Picking it up, she read the display and saw it was Dezra.

"What's..."

"We have a tail, and I don't mean the ones we have in our wolf forms. Onyx wanted me to tell you we will meet you at the old creepy cabin in the swamp out back of your house."

"How the hell are we going to get there?"

"Take the dirt road past your driveway. Drive about a hundred and fifty feet, then hide the SUV in the bushes with the Spanish moss. Then take the overgrown path to the left, which will take you to the cabin. We will meet you there."

Then the line went dead.

"Did you catch all that?" she asked Demon.

"Yeah. Don't panic...but we have a tail as well. They started following about ten minutes ago. Before we can go to the cabin, we need to lose them. You just got rehabilitated, so buckle up."

For once, Kayah didn't argue, "Can you tell how many there are?" she asked as her body started to vibrate.

"When their SUV was close enough, I saw two."

"How many did you and my brother kill when they came after us last time? So it's stupid they would only send two."

"Baby, I think they are just lookouts. I don't think they will try anything, but we don't want them to know our every move either."

"Okay, what is your plan to shake them off our trail?"

"We are going to turn on our road here in a minute so you can get in the glove box and get the Glock. When I tell you to, lean out the window and shoot the tires."

"Sounds like a plan to me."

"Kayah?"

"What?"

"Please listen to me and only shoot the tires. This is not the time for your vengeance."

"Demon, I know...I promise I won't shoot anything but the tires. But I will tell you when it is time. No one will talk me out of taking vengeance for my parents," she said, loading a bullet into the chamber.

"I know...when that time comes, I will be there with you."

As Demon sped down the back roads, sweat pooled at the base of Kayah's spine. When Demon turned the corner onto her street, the tires squealed. She opened the window and hung out just enough to see when the other SUV started to turn the corner. Lifting the Glock, she aimed and pulled the trigger. When the bullet hit the tire, it caused the SUV to barrel roll off the road into the swamp. When Kayah was safely back in the window, Demon hammered the gas making the SUV's engine whine. He slowed down just enough to make the turn onto the dirt road and turned off the headlights. Demon used his wolf night vision to navigate the windy dirt road into the swamps.

When they found where to hide the SUV Kayah jumped out and let Demon back it between the trees. They quickly covered the vehicle with limbs and Spanish moss; then, they took the left path down to the old cabin.

In the cabin, Dezra paced, wondering if Kayah and Demon were okay. She was fine until she heard the gunshot and the sound of a vehicle crashing. When the door to the cabin opened, she was ready to fight until she saw who it was.

"Jesus christ, Kayah! What the fuck happened out there?" Dezra asked, wrapping her arms around her.

"We needed to lose our tail, so I shot one of their tires, sending their SUV into the swamp. D, calm down. We are okay."

The girls watched as the guys did their handshake and one-arm hug, slapping each other on the back.

"So...what made you think of coming here?" asked Kayah looking around.

"Welcome to one of my hideouts...Mi Casa Su Casa," Onyx said, opening his arm to the room.

"Dude, how long have you been staying here?" asked Kayah.

"I started staying here shortly after you bought your house. This was the only way I could stay close to keep you safe without you finding out."

"That's kinda creepy and kinda cool all at the same time. So in a way, I was never alone."

"No, little sister... you were never alone. I would run with you and Demon every night. I always watched your back without you knowing it."

"This is all fine and dandy, but what will we do about the Hunters? They may have only been lookouts tonight. The next time they might do more," Dezra asked, popping the invisible bubble in the room.

"We can work on that in the morning. We still have a few

hours before sunrise. So Kayah, Demon, you can take the guest room. Dezra, you can have my room."

"Where are you going to sleep?" Dezra asked.

"I will sleep on the couch. All of you, please make yourselves at home. The kitchen is stocked, and I changed all the bedding when we arrived. Let's all try and get some sleep. I have an alarm system set up outside. We will know if anyone gets close."

"I am cool with everything except you sleeping on the couch. So you can sleep in the bedroom with me. But we will not be jumping the broom."

"I don't mind sleeping on the couch and letting you have the bed."

"Listen, you are going to learn something quickly. You may have the Alpha bloodline, but I have a mouth and a brain. So any wolf that has claimed me to be his will be brave enough to sleep next to me and control himself."

Onyx smirked, "Yes, mam."

"See, Babe. I told you they were perfect for each other."

"You were right," Demon laughed, rocking back on his heels.

"Go to bed She-Bitch," Dezra said as she stomped.

As Kayah sat on the bed to pull off her pants, "You know it is kinda cool that Onyx was living this close to me."

"Yeah, it is," Demon said as he lifted the covers and extended his arm, inviting Kayah to cuddle in.

Kayah laid her head on Demon's chest and yawned, "You know I envisioned our wedding night going completely different."

"Me too, baby...me too."

Demon moved his hand to her hip, getting comfortable when he heard his sleepy Alpha.

"Don't think about it, buddy. We are not having sex in my brother's swamp cabin for the first time."

Demon chuckled, "I wouldn't think about it. I was getting comfortable. Go to sleep, wife."

When she didn't respond and her breathing changed,

he knew Kayah was sleeping. Demon lay there in the dark, keeping watch so Kayah could sleep. Sleeping was something new to Kayah. She had always run on only a few hours of sleep all her life. When he started to run with her at night, he felt like he could barely function the next day. But Kayah was always bright-eyed and full of energy. Slowly Demon's eyes became too heavy to keep open, so when they finally closed, he was asleep almost instantly.

Chapter 18

She stretched when the sun started streaming through the window, making Demon tighten his grip.

"It's early. Go back to sleep," Demon grumbled.

"Demon, there are things that must be done, and plans must be made."

"A man can dream, can't he?"

"Yes, he can. But think, when all this is done, we will have every morning to sleep in."

"Well, that is something to look forward to."

Just as Demon pinned Kayah to the bed and started kissing her, his phone rang. He picked up his phone and checked the display, "It's my mom." As soon as he answered the phone, he heard the wailing.

"Mom...Mom...Mom, calm down. I can't understand you."

"It's your dad. He…He…He's in the ICU."

"What the fuck do you mean? What happened?"

"He was dumped on the clubhouse, beaten half to death with a big H carved in his chest. Demon, the doctors don't know if he will make it."

"Kayah and I are on our way. I am calling Sid to come and sit with you."

"He is here already."

"Don't leave that hospital. You stay next to Sid. That is an order from your Alpha."

"Demon, the Hunters are gone by now."

"Chloe…OBEY!" Demon barked.

"Yes, Alpha."

While Demon was talking to his mom, Kayah told Onyx and Dezra what had happened. They insisted on going to the hospital and decided to ride with Demon and Kayah.

They found Chloe sitting beside Colby's bed with her head on it and holding his battered hand. The bitter taste of anger sat in the back of Kayah's throat. This is the second father they tried to take from her. Kayah walked into the room, wrapped her arms around Chloe, and held her tight while Demon talked to the doctor.

"Chloe, they will pay for this, I promise."

"Kayah, there has to be a way to solve this without any more violence."

"They are doing this because they want me. They will never stop until they have me or all are dead," Kayah explained.

"Why would they want you?"

"Because of my bloodline. They want to make me a baby factory to make theirs stronger."

"I will kill every one of those son-of-a-bitches. No one is going to touch my wife," Demon growled.

"What did the doctors say?" asked Kayah.

"Dad has massive internal bleeding; both legs are broken,

and they had to remove a piece of Dad's skull because his brain was swelling. The next twenty-four to forty-eight hours are the most critical. After that, he has a chance if he can make it through the surgeries."

"He will pull through...he has to. They can't take another father from me. Plus, Colby needs to be around for his grandkids. Chloe, please stay with Sid. I don't want anything happening to you," Kayah commanded gently.

"Are you asking as my Alpha or as my daughter?"

"Both...but mainly as your daughter."

"Then I will do as you ask."

"Thank you," said Kayah as she hugged Chloe one last time.

Before Kayah followed the others out of the room, Kayah stood next to Colby's bed. Then, as two tears slid down her cheeks, she whispered, "Please hang in there, Dad. You have grandchildren in your future to play with," She kissed his bruised cheek and hurried out of the room.

Kayah paced her living room floor feeling like a caged animal. "I say the first thing we must do is learn who these fuckers are. We need to know everything about them."

"Kayah, what do you want to know?" asked Onyx

"What are their names? Where do they live? Where do they work? Do they have families?"

"I will work on that," said Onyx pulling out a laptop.

"You know something is bothering me," Dezra said out of the blue.

"What is that?" they all asked in unison.

"How did they know last night was yall's wedding? We kept the details quiet. The only ones that knew were pack members. There were so many wolves there. Do we know if they were all our wolves? I am sure we would know the faces of the Dire Wolves, but how do we know that all the other wolves were Timberwolves? It would have been easy for one of those gray wolf bastards to blend in with the Timberwolves. That would answer everything about how they knew where you live. They would also have access to all the information about your wedding. If they had been there last night, they would have known when you and Demon left the clubhouse. They would have also learned when Colby was the most vulnerable."

"That makes a lot of sense, Dezra." Kayah agreed.

"How will we ever find out who it is?" asked Dezra.

"Well, my chocolate bunny...Nyko was known as a legendary Alpha because he knew every one of his wolves. He kept a ledger of all wolves in his office. The ledger had the names of all the families and the bloodlines they came from."

"How many others know about the ledger?" asked Demon.

"No one. He always kept the ledger quiet. I don't even think Mom knew about it."

"Then how do you know about it?" Dezra asked.

"Before I was taken...I woke up because I had to use the bathroom and saw the light in Dad's office. So naturally, I went in to see what Dad was doing, so he sat me on his lap and told me about the ledger and how I would need it when I became

Alpha."

"I think I remember Dad working in a book. If I remember correctly, it is black leather with pictures of the different phases of the moon on it, and it says *New Moon* on the front."

"That would be the one. The only problem is I don't know where in the office he kept it."

"I do...I remember sitting with Dad every night when he worked on the book. So it looks like we are taking a trip to Baton Rouge...I am going home."

Kayah took the next few hours to gather the stuff they needed for the trip. She remembered the wooden box under her father's leather the night Colby gave it to her.

"Go ahead and load this stuff. I will be right back," Kayah told the others.

Demon watched Kayah as she pulled down the hideaway stairs to the attic; she climbed them and disappeared.

"Demon!" called Kayah.

"Yea. What ya need, Babe?"

"Come grab this so I can come down, please."

When Kayah saw him at the bottom of the stairs, she tossed the box to Demon. He studied the box. It was engraved with her father's name and the different phases of the moon carved on the lid. He knew from the craftsmanship that his dad had crafted and carved this box. But, respecting Kayah's privacy, he refused to open the box before she did. Instead, he waited for her to climb back down and handed it back to her. Demon followed Kayah back to the kitchen and watched as she opened the wooden box to reveal her father's Glock and shoulder harness.

A look of resolve washed over Kayah's face when she slipped the shoulder harness into place and adjusted the straps, which fit her like a glove. Demon studied the Alpha that rules by his side as Kayah handled the 9mm Glock like a pro. She packed the extra clips on the right side of the black leather harness and secured the Glock on the left. After she slipped on her father's MC leather, she looked at him and said, "Okay, Demon, I'm ready to go home."

Part Three:

Justice

"Justice will not be served until those who are unaffected are as outraged as those who are."
— Benjamin Franklin

Chapter 19

Onyx stared at Kayah as she descended the stairs. She no longer looked like his baby sister. Kayah's looks had always been a mixture of their parents, but now she reminded him of their father. She has grown into the Alpha their father wanted.

"Sis, the only thing missing from your new ensemble is Dad's bike."

"Whooo, She-Bitch, you look badass."

"I am ready to open a can of whoop-ass. But, then they will know FUCKING with my family and my wolves is fatal," Kayah said as she jumped in the passenger seat of the SUV. Just before she slammed the door, she yelled, "Come on, let's hit the road. Daylight is wasting."

Dezra jumped in the back seat and shut the door, "How long is the drive?"

"We will be on the road about an hour and a half to two hours, depending on how fast Demon drives," Onyx snickered.

"Shut the fuck up!" grumbled Demon causing everyone to laugh.

Everyone stayed to their thoughts during most of the drive.

Demon: *I hope Kayah is mentally ready for this step she is taking into her past. God knows she is strong, but a lot has hit her lately. I am ready for all this to be over with so we can start our life. I need to check with Sid and find out how Dad is doing. They will pay for what they have done to my family.*

Dezra: *Now that Kayah and Demon are our Alphas, what will happen to the MC clubs? Or who is going to run them? Also, I wonder what Kayah will do with her parent's house. Finally, when this is over, will Onyx still be mine? God, that sexy white boy makes all parts of my body pitter-patter whenever I look at him. I don't understand how he can be so open with me about everything yet stay so closed off. I will need to break down those walls carefully. I hope if Onyx is truly the one for me, we will have a love that will last a lifetime.*

Onyx: *I know this is going to be rough for Kayah. I may have been able to clean up the living room; Kayah said she saw everything that night. I know she will get a flashback from hell; if I could take it away, I would. I will take Kayah and Demon up on their offer and become a pack member. Then I can officially make Dezra mine. God only knows how she makes me feel; she has brought my soul back to life. She is sexy, intelligent, confident, and loyal and has a body made for sin. Last night, when I held her when she slept, the darkness that consumed me was gone. Plus, when she starts running her smart mouth, my dick twitches, and my lips tingle when I think about how her lips taste. I can't wait for the day to call her my wife.*

Kayah: *I need to get a handle on my nerves; the closer we get, the more my insides shake. Am I strong enough to walk through the front door of my childhood home? The nightmares are better, but I still hear my mother's screams and my father's weeping. I can still smell the excitement of the men that raped my mother. If I close my eyes, I can still see the pools of blood, and the faces of the men are seared into my brain. I want to be strong enough to walk in and do what I came for. I am ready to start a new chapter of my life with Demon. I want the white picket fence, children, and family BBQs. I want the All-American dream. I want Colby to live and see him playing with his grandchildren. It's weird that I was ready to live as a lone wolf just a few months ago, but now I am fighting for a family. I wonder if Demon would object to Colby being president and patching over my father's MC club. I have a feeling that Onyx will ask me what I plan on doing with our parent's house. I don't have the answers yet.*

Demon's voice broke the silence, "Kayah, how are you doing?"

"My nerves are a little rattled, but I'm good. How close are we?"

"We are about ten minutes out," Onyx answered. "I know it probably won't matter, but the house was cleaned."

"It helps a little. We will see."

∞∞∞

When they pulled into the driveway, the echoes of her mother's screams started bouncing around in her head. Then, with her eyes trained on the front door, she climbed out of the SUV. The giant oak door with the mosaic glass with a wolf howling at a full moon didn't seem so big anymore. Kayah was gripping the house keys so tight they had cut her hand, causing Onyx's nostrils to flare from the scent of fresh blood.

"Kayah, your bleeding," Onyx said, gripping her wrist.

"What?" she said in a daze.

"Here, let me see your hand," Demon said softly.

Kayah opened her hand palm up and stared at the keys lying in a small pool of blood. Demon took the keys, and Dezra doctored Kayah's hand to stop the bleeding.

"We can wait a few minutes if you need," Dezra offered.

"No, I need to do this quick. I think it will be better after I get through the shock," Kayah said, taking back the keys.

Kayah walked to the front door and placed her hand on the door, saying a silent prayer for strength. The key slid into the lock like a hot knife through butter, turned easily, and sounded with a slight click. She expected the door's hinges to squeak, but it opened soundlessly. The house smelled dusty and uninhabited. Kayah stepped through the door and looked around the living room. The bloody couch was gone, and so was the area rug she loved to sit on and play with her dolls, waiting for her dad to come home. Unfortunately, the Christmas tree and the stool for Santa's cookies were still up. She allowed one tear to escape before she wiped it away and pushed the memories away.

Kayah walked over to the hideaway her father had made and pushed the panel so the door would swing open. She squatted down, reached in, and grabbed the bear she slept with every night. She turned and tossed it to Dezra, "Make sure this goes with us." Without asking questions, Dezra searched for a duffel bag to collect anything Kayah wanted to take. Kayah went to the end of the hallway to her father's office. When she turned the doorknob to find it locked, she pulled out her father's keys and tried every one, but none fit.

"Fuck," Kayah said as she hit the door with her fist.

"Now, what are we going to do?" Dezra asked.

"I could always shoot the lock," suggested Kayah.

"That is not a good idea."

"Why?"

"Because a gunshot can be heard. We are trying to stay under the radar," stated Demon.

"Well, how the hell are we going to get in there then?"

"Kayah, I know this will be rough for you, but I must ask some questions. The night our parents were killed, did Dad use his office?" asked Onyx.

"No."

"Okay, I need you to remember what you did that day."

"Why does that matter?" asked Demon.

"Because without Kayah realizing it, Dad could have hidden

the key, and she could know where it is."

"Yes, I remember that day very well. It was Christmas Eve, and Dad left to go to the clubhouse like he did every morning after he ate breakfast with Mom and me. Then Mom and I played and had a tea party. Mom told me that after my nap, we could bake cookies for Santa and make dinner for Dad. I remember Mom getting a phone call from Dad saying he would be late for dinner, so Mom put his plate in the microwave. Then we decorated cookies and put a plate out for Santa. After that, I asked her to turn on the Christmas tree lights, and Dad came home. I didn't want to go to bed, so Dad held me until I fell asleep. I don't remember who put me to bed; I woke up from Mom's screams. I went to my hiding spot that Dad made, and you all know the rest."

"What about her father's leather?" asked Dezra.

"A leather vest is not going to unlock the door, dingbat," Kayah said, shaking her head.

"No, smart one, did you look for a hidden or tiny pocket?"

"Huh..." Kayah said, searching every inch of the leather.

Kayah ran her hands on the flat part of the leather. When she found nothing, she moved to the seems. Then, on the left side, almost to the bottom of the leather, she felt something hard, and after inspecting it, she saw the stitching didn't match the rest of the leather.

"Here, use this," Dezra offered.

Kayah took the nail file from Dezra and started pulling the stitching out. She pulled out a piece of folded paper when she had made a whole big enough. Kayah unfolded the paper to find a key tucked away. She fisted the key tightly and said, "It is a letter from my Dad."

Chapter 20

"What does it say, Kai?" asked Demon.

"Do you want me to read it?" Onyx asked.

She shook her head no before reading it aloud.

Kayah,

My baby girl! I am so proud of you. You are my pride and joy. But, unfortunately, if you are reading this, I have passed on, and you have ascended into your powers. Your mom and I never meant to leave you. You need to know some things, and I am sorry I am not there to teach you. By now, I am sure Colby told you that you are exceptionally special. I will start by telling you a story that began long ago. Your great, great, great grandfather came from a place called Aadya. He was the beginning of our ancient bloodline, and his name was Vesper. Vesper was the Alpha of the Timberwolves in Aadya.

The Gods of Aadya found out that the realm was to be cursed. So the Goddess Artemis devised a plan to help the wolves survive. First, she imbued our blood with magic, and that is when we gained the ability to live as humans and shift into wolves at will. After she gave the wolves their new abilities, she opened portals; you would know them as shimmers from bedtime stories. The portals opened here; the name of this realm is Edan. You, my beautiful princess, are the first Omega wolf born in two hundred years. Omegas are chosen by the gods, which makes you very rare. When you ascended, you gained the abilities of a werewolf without the bloodlust. This is how you can be an Alpha.

You also need to know that you are not an only child. You have or had a brother; his name is Onyx. Your brother disappeared when he was little, and your mother and I believe he was taken by one of the dark creatures from Aadya that snuck through one of the portals. When he couldn't be found, this world thought him dead… but your mother and I never gave up looking for him. Your sibling bond will activate if he is alive when you shift for the first time.

The bond between siblings is powerful and unique.

The next danger you will need to know about is the Hunters; they are gray wolves. They want to mix our bloodlines to strengthen them; if that ever happened, it would be catastrophic here and in Aadya. So you must make sure they never combine the bloodlines. You will find all the information you need in my office. The key that was wrapped up in this letter is the key you will need to unlock my office. I hope you found the key before breaking down the door. If you find my office open, the information you need is in the false wall safe. You know the bedtime story to open the lock.

I love you, princess! Mine and your mother's hope for you is to live a full and happy life full of family and children.

Love,
Daddy

∞∞∞

Kayah folded the letter and slid it into the back pocket of her jeans. She unlocked the office door and stepped inside. Kayah could tell the office had gone untouched for years; it was just as she remembered.

"Well, let's get started. Gather anything you think will help."

Kayah went straight to the desk; she pulled open the top drawer. Then, reaching in, she felt for the hidden button that would open the false wall. The panel slid into the wall with no sound. Demon followed Kayah into the secret room and gawked at the safe. The safe door was the size of the wall. There was a hand pressure plate and an LCD screen.

Kayah pressed her hand to the hand plate, and the screen lit up, and spoke.

Computer: ...Hello Kayah...To gain entry, you must be able to answer the questions correctly. You may enter the answers by voice or typing. How would you like to respond?

"Voice," answered Kayah.

Computer: ...You chose the voice command. All of your answers will be recorded by voice. Are you ready to start?

"Yes."

Computer: Question one...Where did your bloodline come

from?

"Aadya."

Computer: Correct. Question two...When is a wolf the strongest?

"During a Full Moon."

Computer: Correct. Question three...What is the name of the Goddess that gave you your powers?

"Artemis."

Computer: What are you?

"I am a Timberwolf Alpha that was born an Omega."

Computer: Correct. Question four...Who are you to Nyko?

"His daughter."

Computer: Incorrect. Would you like me to repeat the question?

"Yes."

Computer: Question four...Who are you to Nyko?

Before she could answer, Demon leaned over and whispered, "Try, princess."

Nodding, she looked at Demon when she answered, "His princess."

Computer: Correct. Access granted. Welcome home, Kayah.

When the lock sounded, Demon placed his palms on the door and pushed. The door swung open. Kayah gaped at the contents of the room. On one side of the room was an arsenal that could weaponize an entire army. On the other side were shelves with file folders with names and years.

"Demon, will you go find Onyx, please."

"Ahh, yeah...be right back."

Kayah listened to the murmurs of the others talking while she walked further into the room. She was looking at the files when the others came back.

"Whoo...She-Bitch, your daddy was a scary man. Are you sure he wasn't the bad guy?"

"I had no idea that Dad even had this room. Did you, Kayah?"

"Umm...No."

"Then how did you know where the button was?" Demon

asked.

"When I was little, I saw it when I was sitting on my dad's lap. I wanted to push it, and he told me he would show me what it would do when I was older. The safe I was talking about is the bottom drawer of the desk. I was secretly hoping the button would open that panel. I remember Dad saying he didn't want to work with the Hunters because they were illegal gun and drug runners. So I have no idea why he has all these guns and files. Onyx, who was our Dad?"

"I have no idea, baby sister, but we will find out."

"Hey Kayah, come check this out; there are a bunch of journals over here," called Dezra.

"Pack them up. We will take them with us. Demon, Onyx, will you pack up the guns and ammo? Dezra, help me gather the binders that you think will be any help. I am going to get the ledger we came after," Kayah said, walking back to the desk.

Kayah sat at her father's desk and opened the false drawer to reveal the safe. Looking at the dial, she remembered the story her dad told her to open the safe.

*"Daddy and Mommy met when they were **eighteen** years old. They had two children, but now they were down to **one**. When she turns **twenty-one**, she will have an army to call her own.* As she turned the combination dial, she called out the numbers.

"Left eighteen…right one…left twenty-one."

She turned the handle and pulled the safe door open. Inside, she found the ledger, a hundred thousand dollars, passports, and new identifications. She quickly cleaned out the safe while calling for Dezra.

"D, you still got room in that bag?"

"Yes, what's up?"

"I have some stuff to put in it. We need to hurry. We have been here too long. They will know we are here if this place is being watched."

"I agree; be sure you lock up this room and the office," said Demon.

Kayah ensured her father's office was secure when they had everything they needed. After they loaded the SUV, they backed down the driveway. They decided to stay in a hotel instead of driving back to New Orleans. Before checking into the hotel, they drove around for about an hour to make sure no one followed them.

Chapter 21

After they ordered food and checked into their rooms, Kayah settled down with one of her dad's journals.

April 5th

This is my first entry; it has been five days since Onyx disappeared. I searched the woods and only found one set of footprints in the mud. How can there be footprints but no scent to follow? Ashseara is in mourning for the loss of our son. She has stayed in bed for five days.

April 10th

I expanded my search and found more of the same footprints, but a human's body was with them this time. The police said the man was drained of all his blood; there were no cuts or wounds on the body except for two puncture wounds on the neck. In my grandfather's notes, I have read about creatures that live only on human blood. Could one of these creatures be what took my baby boy?

April 20th

I am convinced this is one of the creatures I have read about. They came from the same place we wolves came from. It is a place called Aadya. Some of these vile creatures must have escaped when the wolves were fleeing. The police have given up the search for Onyx, but I have not. I know my son is still alive...I will find him or die trying.

September 15th

It has been a while since my last entry. I have been learning about the creatures and how to kill them. The creatures are called vampires; they can survive on any blood but prefer humans. I can smell the change on Ashseara; I know she is pregnant. I need to protect my family, and I plan to build a safe room off of my office.

February 3rd

We found out that Ashseara is having a girl. We have decided to name her Kayah. I still go out every night looking for my son or any leads pointing me in the right direction to the creature that took him. The safe room is complete, and I have started filling it with guns and special ammo to protect my family.

June 16th

Kayah was born today; she is perfect in every way. She has the prettiest eyes I have ever seen. They have an electric blue ring in them. I have reinforced our home because I found the footprints close to the house again. It has already taken my son. But, it will not take my princess.

June 20th

I came face-to-face with the creature tonight; it was looking in Kayah's window. By the time I made it outside, it was gone. I will find a priest to come out and bless our land. I heard vampires couldn't walk on holy ground, but I will need more research.

August 15th

Today is Onyx's 5th birthday. Happy birthday son! Ashseara has been busy with our little princess, but I can see the sorrow in her eyes over our son. This is the second birthday he has been gone.

It is okay, my beloved. We will get through this…I will find my son.

December 24

Tomorrow is Christmas, and a full moon. Kayah is showing signs that she is an Omega. Colby and I have agreed that his son Demon and Kayah will be mated. Demon and Kayah will bridge the gap between the packs. My princess will become Alpha to the Timberwolves.

June 16th

Today is Kayah's 1st birthday. Last night I know I heard my son howl at the moon for the first time. I know I am close to finding some of the answers. Somehow the secret that Kayah is an Omega has leaked. The Alpha of the Gray Wolves (Hunters) has asked me to make a pack for his son and her to be mated. I will never let Kayah be associated with that pack. The Hunters are a rogue pack that runs guns and drugs. They have no regard for following pack laws.

It was almost midnight when Demon slid into bed next to Kayah, "Anything interesting?"

Kayah closed the journal and rubbed her eyes, "Yes, actually. The letter was right. My parents never gave up looking for Onyx. It said that my Dad said he heard Onyx howl at the moon the night before my first birthday."

"What does that mean?" he asked.

"Think about it…it means that Onyx was only five when he shifted for the first time. It makes me wonder, did I shift for the first time because of the trauma of my parents being killed? Or was it time for my first shift because of my bloodline? Timberwolf pups shift for the first time around their sixteenth birthday. There are many questions without answers."

"Baby, we will search for the answers. But for now, put it all away; let that busy brain rest."

"My brain is racing; I don't know if I can shut it off."

"See, that I can help with," Demon said, covering her mouth with his.

Kayah forgot about her father's journal as it slid off the bed onto the floor. When Demon ran his hands up her sides, he brushed the sides of her breast, causing her breath to shudder.

"I have waited years to get my hands on you," murmured Demon between kisses.

Kayah has always loved Demon; she fell in love with him when they were sixteen. He still made her stomach flutter every time he looked at her. And he was hers by human and pack law.

The scent of Kayah's arousal pulled out the Primal Alpha that lay dormant deep inside Demon. Demon sniffed the air and growled; he gripped the collar of her tee shirt and gave an effortless pull ripping the shirt down the center, leaving her breathless. Demon went to work on her pants, leaving her only in a bra and panties.

"God, you are beautiful. I know I have seen you naked a hundred times when we are shifting, but tonight feels different."

Demon started at her toes, licking and kissing his way up her body; when he reached the apex of her thighs, he placed a small kiss and then continued his way up her body. Demon placed a kiss between her breasts and squeezed them just hard enough to where he could feel her nipples harden in his palms. With one continuous lick, he moved to her neck, snaking his hand to the back of her hair; he fisted a handful and pulled, exposing Kayah's neck. Then he sank his teeth into her flesh at the crook of her neck and shoulder, just hard enough to be on the edge of pain, making Kayah moan in pure bliss. Kayah heard the click of Demon's pocket knife then he whispered, "I hope you're not overly fond of these."

Then he took the knife and cut her bra between the cups. He bit down on her hard nipple, making her back bow off the bed. Before she could object, he cut the strings on her silk panties and bit her on the hip leaving teeth marks. As Kayah discarded the destroyed clothing, Demon undressed, never taking his eyes off her. Demon reached down and gripped Kayah by her ankles, pulling her to the bed's end and placing her thighs over his shoulders. He locked his arms around the small of her back, lifted her into the air, and walked over to put her back against the wall. When he knew she was safely secure, he buried his face in the delta between her legs, making Kayah scream in ecstasy when she came. He carefully switched his hold on her when she went limp and carried her back to the bed. Demon flipped her on her stomach and lifted her to her knees by her hips.

"Grab the bars on the headboard," Demon growled.

Kayah looked back at him and asked," What?"

"You may be an Alpha that rules by my side. But, in the bedroom, that is a different story. In here, I am your Alpha. You will submit and obey," he said as he landed a hard smack on her ass, making it pink. "Now be a good girl and do as your told. Grab the bars, and don't let go until you are told."

Kayah quickly discovered she was not moving fast enough when three more smacks landed on her pink cheeks. As soon as she had a grip on the bars, Demon wrapped his hand into Kayah's hair and pulled her head, tipping it back and making her back bow, moving her hips in the correct position. Demon claimed his mate with one powerful push and completed the par bond. After Kayah came, Demon emptied himself into her and slowly withdrew. With the primal Alpha sated, Demon rubbed her pink ass cheeks and said softly, "You can let go, baby."

When she let go of the bars, Demon helped her roll onto her back. Kayah watched as he gently crawled between her legs, then laid atop her and cradled her face in his hands. Kayah wrapped her legs around his waist, and when Demon kissed her, he gently pushed inside, making love to his wife.

Kayah watched her sleeping mate through sated eyes when their lovemaking was done. It wasn't long before she fell into a dreamless sleep.

Chapter 22

The following day Kayah and Demon woke to Dezra pounding on the door and yelling.

"SHE-BITCH OPEN THE DOOR. PUT SOME FUCKING CLOTHES ON AND OPEN THE GODDAMN DOOR!"

Kayah stood, slipped Demon's tee shirt over her head, and answered the door.

"What the hell is the emergency?"

"Girl let me in...I found out who the traitor is."

"Well, don't leave us in suspense. Who the hell is it?"

"It's Bear."

"There is no way. We grew up with him. Bear is one of my best friends," argued Demon.

"Demon, listen to me...I know what I know. I read it in the ledger. Nyko had a roster of all three wolf packs. Bear is the Alpha's son. He was raised as an orphan, just like Kayah," explained Dezra.

"Fuck that means they knew Kayah was alive the whole time. They wanted to ensure Kayah was indeed the Omega and for her to ascend. Now what the fuck are we going to do?" yelled Demon.

Demon and Dezra watched as Kayah paced, not saying a word. Finally, after ten minutes, Demon asked, "Dezra, go get Onyx."

"K," she said, running out the door.

When Dezra returned with Onyx, she said, "See, that is all she does."

"Dude, you broke my sister. Did you bang the smarts right out of her?"

"No, She just found out that one of our friends is the leak to The Hunters," Demon spat.

Onyx's casual stance changed, "Who?"

"It's Bear."

"Who is he?" asked Onyx.

"He is the son of the Gray Wolves Alpha. One of the fuckers that killed our parents and raped our mother," Kayah said bitterly.

"How was he able to get that close to you?"

"The pack raised him as an orphaned wolf," Dezra explained.

"I read in Dad's journal last night that the Alpha of the Gray Wolves wanted Dad to promise me to his son. But Dad turned him down, and that is what led to the death of our parents."

"I remember when we were in high school, Bear commenting on how he would make you his. I was already in love with you by then. I didn't like him staking a claim on you, so I beat his ass. That's why I got suspended for two weeks," Demon said as he rubbed his bald head.

"So what do we do know?" Dezra asked.

"By pack law, he has betrayed the pack, and its Alphas, and the sentence for betrayal is death," Demon explained.

"You know, I had noticed that Bear was missing after

the pack meeting when you took over being Alpha of the Timberwolves. He was not at the wedding. That would also explain how The Hunters know where Colby and Chloe live," Kayah said.

"Sweetness, did the ledger have the addresses of wolf members?" Onyx asked Dezra.

"It has some of the addresses, but many said the location is unknown," she answered.

"Okay, Kayah, What do you want to do?" Onyx asked.

We can't play it safe all the time, so I think it's time we head to Lafayette. The first person I want to track down is Bear. He is top on my list."

"Baby, I won't stand in your way, but I will pull rank if necessary. Bear is mine! He betrayed my pack before they were combined. He is why my father is in the hospital on the brink of death. As Alpha of the Dire Wolves, I stake my claim for the right to carry out the judgment on Bear."

"I understand, but if you are going to do this per pack law, there needs to be a trial," Kayah added.

"Understood," was all Demon said.

"What wolves can you trust to help without alerting Bear to what we are doing?" asked Onyx.

"Shilo, Sid… I don't know," Demon said, shaking his head.

"Would Sid know?" Dezra asked.

"Yes. But he is on guard duty at the hospital," said Demon.

"I can call the hospital and have security in your dad's room," Dezra suggested.

"Yes. I completely forgot about that. Randle is head of security. He will do anything for Dezra and me," Kayah chimed in.

"That is a good idea. You call the hospital, and I will call Sid. Onyx, take an inventory of the guns we recovered at your parent's house; we may need to arm an army," said Demon.

Everyone went their way to put plans into motion. Then,

after all the calls were made, all they could do was wait. Kayah read more journal entries, Onyx made sure they had enough weapons and ammo, and Demon and Dezra read through the binders taken from the safe room.

July 30th

Things are getting rough with The Hunters. First, I discovered that the vampire that took Onyx works closely with the Gray Wolves. I also found that the Gray Wolves were the only ones who served a witch in Aadya named Surana. So I was right—they are from the dark parts of Aadya. I have hidden the secret to helping my son if I ever find him inside Kayah's favorite stuffed animal.

"Holy fuck..."

"What?" they all said in unison.

"Dezra, did you bring my bear?"

"Yes...why?"

"Toss it here."

Dezra tossed the bear at Kayah with a puzzled look. Kayah examined the bear and noticed that the stitching on his left foot was messed up.

"Demon, Can I use your pocket knife, please?"

Kayah used the knife and cut the stitching enough to fit her finger and thumb. Then, after feeling around for a couple of minutes, she felt something hard. Kayah pulled out a piece of paper folded to the size of a quarter. She unfolded the paper and read.

Kayah, my princess,

If you ever find your brother, you have the power to cure him. Of course, it isn't a complete cure, but it will cure him all the same. All he needs to do is drink some of your blood. You must trust and believe he will have the strength to stop. I will warn you now; the bloodlust he has is very strong. This will allow him to be like you; he will keep all his super abilities and still needs to drink blood to survive, but the blood lust will disappear.

Love always,

Daddy.

"Onyx, you need to read this; it's from our father," she said, handing him the paper.

"What is it?" he asked.

Everyone watched in silence as Onyx read the letter. When he was done, he looked at his sister and said, "NO. The fucking answer is no."

"Why? It can set you free."

"What did the letter say?" Dezra asked.

"It doesn't matter. Because it will never happen."

"It says that my blood can cure him. It will take away the blood lust from drinking blood," Kayah answered her.

"I have known about this cure. The one thing Dad didn't tell you is that I need to feed off of you. I can't drink the blood out of a cup," he said bitterly.

Onyx stood, not knowing what to do. His heart was torn in two. He wanted to accept help from his sister so he could live an everyday life, but on the other hand, he knew the blood lust was too strong. He would never be able to stop; he could kill his sister.

"So, and? Onyx, you are my brother, and I trust you."

"Fucking drop it, Kayah! I said no."

"Tell me why? Why won't you let me help you?"

"When the blood lust starts, it is too hard for me to control. The blood lust controls me. I don't want to be responsible for killing my sister and one of the pack's Alphas."

"You drank from me and were able to stop," said Demon.

"That was different."

"How is it different if you drink from him and you won't drink from me?"

"I had just been in a huge fight and was injured. Plus, your blood will taste different; it would be like a drug to me. Kayah, I am trying to be a big brother; I am trying to protect you."

A knock sounded on the door, "We are not done with this conversation," Kayah said, crossing the room to open the door.

Sid walked into the hotel room and almost stepped back, "What's going on in here? You could cut the tension with a knife."

"Just a disagreement between my brother and me," Kayah said, sitting beside Demon.

"Okay...Tell me what kind of shit you all have stepped in," asked Sid.

"First of all, we would like to thank you for coming out here to help us. Second, this pile of shit is enormous. It started long ago when Onyx was taken," stated Kayah.

"Now let me say... First, of course, I would come; you are my Alpha. Second, I would have come anyway. I helped save and raise your rotten butt," Sid said with a smile.

"It looks like The Hunter had Onyx taken, but the Alpha wanted me to be mated with his son. When my father refused, they killed him and planted his son in our pack as a spy, letting them know everything. That is the short version," explained Kayah letting out a sigh.

"We will get to the other stuff you mentioned. Right now, I want to know who is the trader?"

"Bear."

"FUCK!"

Chapter 23

"I am so sorry," Kayah said, feeling ashamed.

"For what?" Sid asked.

"For bringing these problems into our pack."

"Kayah, stop that shit. It is not your fault that Fuck-Twit betrayed the pack. For fuck sake, he grew up with you guys. He was one of your friends. By pack law, death is the only future he has. So now, how is The Hunter responsible for what happened to Onyx?"

"Are you familiar with the legend?" asked Kayah.

"Yes, every wolf is."

"Okay. Well, in the realm of Aadya, many creatures live there. One of these creatures slipped through the portals and came here. This creature worked with a witch, and so did the Gray wolves. This creature kidnapped my brother, and when he was of age, she turned him into…."

"Are you talking about vampires?"

"Yes."

Sid turned and looked at Onyx, "Cerilla is your maker?"

"How the fuck do you know that?" Onyx growled.

"Chill out. I am not a threat to you. I only know about her because I saw this beautiful woman standing outside Shilo's window one night. When I yelled at her, she hissed and showed her fangs. After that, I started doing research. Then when you were taken, I was with Colby when your Dad told me everything he had found," explained Sid.
"Why didn't you tell me?"

"Kayah, you were treated like an outcast growing up; would you have believed me if I had come to you about this?"

"I guess not."

"So we need to start cleaning up this mess and setting the scales of justice right," Sid said, watching Onyx eat a little Debbie fudge round. "Dude, if you are a vampire, how the hell are you eating snack cakes?"

"Because of my bloodline, she couldn't turn me into that monster. So I am a vampire and a wolf. So I am a hybrid."

"Groovy. Now we need to work on getting the wolves up here, so we can make our next move. We need a place that can hold a couple of hundred wolves."

"We can always use Dad's clubhouse," suggested Onyx.

"That would work, plus it is reinforced. After Onyx was taken, Nyko reinforced everything. Plus, there should be weapons there as well."

"Then I guess we need to get this shindig going and get on the road," Dezra joked, trying to lighten the mood making everyone laugh.

∞∞∞

In a couple of hours, they were safely in the confines of the clubhouse and putting the first part of their plans into action. It only took a few hours before wolves/bikers started showing up. As each wolf or human arrived, they started helping without even asking.

"Sid, why are there humans here?" asked Kayah.

"Because, little lady, we knew this day was coming. Nyko was our MC President, and he informed us that problems were headed his way. At our last meeting, we voted to help you when you became Alpha of the Timberwolves. We wanted a family in the MC to raise you when your parents were killed. But Nyko told us it would be better if a wolf family raised you instead."

"Who are you?"

"Aww, Kayah I'm hurt. You don't remember me?"

"No, I'm sorry," she apologized.

"Well, it has been a long time. I am John, your father's VP."

"No disrespect, but your human."

John grabbed his chest, tipped his head back, and laughed. Kayah watched him until he turned red, tears streaming down his cheeks from laughing. John stood six feet tall and had a slight beer belly. He wore black motorcycle boots, blue jeans, leather riding chaps, a black tee shirt, and a leather vest resembling her Dads.

"Did I say something funny," she asked, a little huffy.

"I'm sorry, Kayah, I am not laughing at you. I have been a part of this group and family for so long that I forget that it is taboo for humans to know about you wolves."

"How did you find out about us?" she asked.

"Well, the easiest way to put it. My old lady Celestria was Ashseara's sister."

"If she were my mother's sister, that would make you my...."

"Uncle."

"So, if you are my uncle, why have I never met you?"

"Because after your parents were killed, The Hunters killed my beloved Celestria. They kept a very close eye on me after that. Colby found ways to tell me how you were doing and get me pictures. I heard you got married, but by pack law, since my wife has passed, I am no longer allowed to attend pack meetings. Nothing short of that would have ever kept me away from you. I never got a chance to have my own children, but I love you like you are mine."

"You know we are getting ready to war with wolves, right?"

"Yes, and so do the other fifty humans in here. We want justice for what happened to our president, his old lady, and my wife. Kayah, I may not be a wolf, but I have the courage and the heart of a wolf. So please let us help."

"You and the rest of the humans are welcome to stay and help. Do the other humans know we are wolves?"

"Yes. The humans that are here are members of your father's MC club. Well, I guess it is your MC now. I have a question for you. After this is done, would you object to patching over the MC with the New Orleans chapter?"

"Put it to a vote. But I know the members would be proud to patch over. I think that was your dad's goal once you became Alpha."

"Now that you mention that, how many of you knew I was an Omega and would be Alpha?"

"All of us. After Onyx was taken, Nyko ensured an army to protect you."

Onyx walked up and slung an arm around his sister's shoulders, and said, "I heard my name."

John stumbled back at the sight of Onyx, "Is that really you?"

The smile fell off Onyx's face, "Uncle John?" Was all he could say before John fisted a hand in his shirt and pulled him into a hug. Kayah stared at the man she now knew was her uncle. He still looked tough and mean, hugging her brother and crying. She took this time to sneak away to go and find her husband, leaving the two of them to catch up on lost time. She found Demon talking with Shilo and Sid in the front of the room. When she was close, Demon looked up and smiled.

"So, you will never guess what just happened to me," she said, leaning into Demon.

"What's that, baby?"

"I just met my very human uncle."

"What the hell did you just say?" asked Shilo.

"My very human uncle was mated/married to my mother's sister. Oh, and get this, he was my father's VP in the MC."

"This shit just keeps getting weirder and weirder," Shilo said, shaking his head.

"I know. Have either of you seen Dezra?"

"Yeah, she is in the kitchen with Taria and some other female wolves and old ladies," Demon said, leaning over to kiss her temple.

"What are they doing?"

"Cooking."

"Why did I even ask?"

∞∞∞

Kayah sat at the head of the table with Demon, Onyx, Dezra, Shilo, Taria, Sid, and John while they ate. Kayah was surprised that so many wolves and humans had come to help them. By the roster that was filled out, three hundred and ninety showed. All of them were willing to put their life on the line to help get justice for their parents. She was having a hard time knowing that not everyone would survive. The only ones that needed to die were the pieces of shit that killed her parents and for what they did to her brother. She was picking up on some of their conversations with her super sonic hearing. She smiled when she heard that Shilo and Taria wanted to be mated. She also picked up on how much Onyx adored Dezra. She heard people talking about Colby and how he was still in the ICU and how it was about time they were able to get justice, not only for her parents but Colby as well. Knowing this was not a family reunion she tapped Demon on the leg, letting him know it was time to call the meeting to order.

Chapter 24

When Kayah and Demon took their spots behind the podium, the low hum of talking stopped. Kayah took a steadying breath while she looked at the faces of her army. Then, when she was calm, she called the meeting to order.

Kayah: *"Wolves of New Orleans and Baton Rouge, I call this meeting to order."*

All Wolves: *"Yes, Alpha."*

Kayah: *"Human bikers, this is a privilege to be allowed to attend this meeting. What you see and hear must be kept to yourselves. Do you agree with this?"*

Bikers: *"Yes!"*

Kayah: *"Let's begin."*

As Kayah conducted the meeting, Demon, Shilo, Tiara, Dezra, and Sid watched the group to see if anything was shady.

Kayah: *"All of you should know by now I am the daughter of Nyko and one of the Alphas of this pack. What I would like to tell you started long ago, before I was born. But, for the humans, I will begin at the very beginning. The wolves came from a place called Aadya."*

When Kayah was done telling the whole story, the place was so quiet you could hear a pin drop. She looked over the group and saw mixed emotions on their faces. The humans were stunned; some wolves were outraged, and some women were crying.

Kayah: *"Before we move on, are there any questions?"*

"I have one," one of the humans said, standing.

Kayah: *"Who are you, and what is your question?"*

"My name is Caleb, but your dad called me Crash. My question is, when do we get this show on the road? I don't care if you are a wolf or a human. No one has the right to do what they did. The second question, we know how to take care of The Hunters but how do we take care of Cerilla?"

Kayah: *"We can't go after her right now. If we do, it will kill my brother. So she is off-limits, just like Bear. If anyone goes after either, they will have me to deal with. Is this understood? I will let you know when it is safe to hunt Cerilla. Is everyone in agreement?"*

Everyone in the room: *"Yes, Alpha."*

"I have a question."

Kayah: *"Who are you, and what is your question?"*

"My name is Charles, and your Dad called me Chuckie. Is it true you can turn us?"

Kayah: *"Into wolves?"*

"Yes."

Kayah: *"No. I can not. That is a myth that was started in story books."*

Onyx: *"I could turn them…but I won't; the bloodlust would be too strong."*

"Kayah, your dad said he had something that could give the humans your strength. He said they were passed down from his grandfather to protect the humans taken in by the pack. But it only works if the humans take the wolf oath and live by pack law for the rest of their lives."

Sid: *"The amulets you are talking about only work if you are mated to a wolf and a partial par bond has been created between you. How many humans are mated to a wolf?"*

Kayah watched as every human raised their hand. Then, stunned, Demon leaned over and whispered into her ear, "Damn, Nyko was not playing around when he said he created an army to protect you and the pack."

Kayah: *"How many of you have gone through the par bond ritual?"*

Once again, Kayah watched as almost every human raised his hand.

Kayah: *"How many humans want to join the wolf pack?"*

All the humans raised their hands.

Kayah: *"The ritual can only happen during a full moon. Tomorrow night is the next full moon. The wolves that are not par-*

bonded will participate in the ritual then all humans will be sworn into the pack. Are there any other questions before I close this meeting?"

Everyone: *"No, Alpha."*

Kayah: *"Then I call this meeting to a close. We have prepared enough sleeping quarters for everyone. This building is reinforced and protected; I suggest you stay here until this war ends."*

When everyone started moving around and finding a place to lay their head, John approached Kayah.

"I never got a chance to join the pack before your aunt was killed," he said sadly.

"Did she par bond to you?" asked Demon.

"Yes, and I have the scar to prove it," he said, stretching his shirt collar to expose the scar from the bite.

"Then welcome to the pack, Uncle," Onyx said with a smile.

Demon watched Kayah as she slept; he knew she was on

edge with so many wolves and humans around her. As she slept, his mind wandered into his own thoughts. *She has always been more comfortable with being alone or with just a select few in her circle around her. These wolves may be members of her pack. There were just too many of them she didn't know yet. That's not even touching the issues she had having humans around. Wolves saw humans as fickle. Tonight they would add humans into their world and their pack. He knew Kayah wanted to protect the humans that were loyal to her father and his pack. Nyko knew this war was coming. Why else would he have let humans so close and learn their secrets? One of these humans was part of Kayah's family. Were humans and wolves even able to have children? And if they did, were they wolf or human? Could they even shift?*

Demon looked down at Kayah; her head lay on his bare chest with her chestnut brown hair fanned over his right shoulder. She had her hand resting on his stomach and her leg over his as if using him as a body pillow. *He had always loved how her tan skin looked against his. Kayah's dark golden tan skin always seemed so light because of his dark chocolate skin. He knew their children would be beautiful; Demon envisioned them having delicate mocha skin, Kayah's brilliant blue eyes, and dark curly soft hair like their mom.* The noise from Demon's phone vibrating on the bedside table pulled Kayah from her slumber. Not wanting to move, she watched Demon check the display with her eyes half closed.

"Huh."

"What, babe? Who is it?"

"Bear."

Kayah sat up in bed, fully alert. "Babe, answer it; I have an idea. But you need to play it off. You don't know anything. He is just our friend."

Demon answered the phone and placed it on speaker so Kayah could hear everything said.

"Hey, brother…What's happening?"

"Nothing, I just got home. What are your plans today?" asked Bear.

Demon looked down at the note Kayah wrote and quickly answered.

"I am at Kayah and Onyx's parent's house," Demon answered as he fisted the blanket to keep his cool.

"Dude, what the fuck are you doing out there?"

"Kayah and Onyx decided to clean and sell the house."

"Why now? Kayah could have done it years ago," commented Bear.

"They are ready for this chapter of their life to be done."

"Man, I can understand that. But do you guys need some help? I can drive up there; it's the least I can do since I missed your wedding." Bear offered.

"Yeah, man, that would help since my dad can't help. The extra set of hands would help out a lot. So why were you missing from the wedding?"

"I told you I had that business trip to Houston. But wait, what is Colby doing that he can't help? So I figured that if anyone helped, it would be Colby. From what I understand,

Colby and Nyko were friends."

"Because my dad is in the ICU fighting for his life."

"What the fuck? What happened?"

"He was jumped the night of our wedding. My dad is in a coma. They don't know if he will make it. When I find the son of a bitches that did this...I will taste their blood as I rip their throat out."

"Count me in. I will help in any way I can."

"Brother, I wouldn't have it any other way," Demon said, smirking while looking at Kayah.

"Alright. Give me twenty minutes, and I will be on the road."

"Sounds good; having a friend here to help will be nice. Kayah is having a hard time being here. See you when you get here," Demon said as he disconnected the call.

Demon was quiet for a few minutes, then he picked up Kayah's hand and kissed it.

"That was good thinking," Demon said softly.

"What's wrong?" asked Kayah.

"I have an internal struggle."

"Why?"

"Because I just lied to one of my oldest friends. Yet I will rejoice when I rip his head off his shoulders and drop the traitor's head at his father's feet."

Chapter 25

Kayah and Demon dressed quickly and went in search of Dezra and Onyx. They were spotted on one of the many couches, Dezra was snuggled up to Onyx reading one of the many binders taken, and he had his nose in his laptop.

"Guys, we need to go."

"What's up, Kai?" Dezra asked.

"Demon just had a conversation with Bear. He is going to meet us at our parent's house to help us clean it out," Kayah explained while doing air quotes.

"Sis, I think we need to take a few wolves with us, just in case he is planning an ambush," suggested Onyx.

"I would not take any humans just yet," Dezra added.

"Why?" asked Demon.

"Because they have not been made part of the pack yet.

Humans are very breakable; they don't have any protection yet," Dezra reminded them.

"See, that's one of the things I love about you. You don't miss any details," Kayah said, smiling.

"Okay, we need to act quickly. We don't know if he is in New Orleans or here. Dezra, will you help Kayah and Demon load the SUV? I will gather some wolves I can trust." asked Onyx.

"Of course, love," answered Dezra as she stood.

Within ten minutes, everyone was in vehicles and on the road. Some wolves ran through the woods; their parent's house was only a few miles from the clubhouse. Kayah tuned into her wolf senses and found out that she could tell where every one of her wolves was at. She had three hiding in the woods to the left, two were behind the house, and two were on the right. She closed her eyes, pictured the wolves in her mind, and sent a message to them.

Wolves, this is your Alpha. Slow your heart rate to make yourself undetectable. Hold your positions unless help is needed.

Remember, Bear's fate belongs to your Alpha. If he gets past us, you are to capture only. So stay safe, my wolves, and watch your six.

"How the hell did you do that?" Dezra asked while rubbing her head.

"I read in one of my father's journals that our ancestors could communicate this way. However, when we were given the gift to shift into a human form, we lost that gift. It was said that the Omega was born in an Alpha bloodline and could give this gift back to any wolf that attended the wedding, and she became Alpha of the pack," she explained.

"What other cool shit did we get from you?" Dezra asked.

"Well, you all got my strength, speed, the ability to half shift, and talk telepathically, you can make yourself undetectable by slowing your heart rate, and you will pass these gifts off to your children. The biggest advantage is that you will be at your strongest three nights out of the month," she said, smiling, rocking back on her heels."

"Would it be the night before, the night of, and the night

after the full moon?" Demon asked.

Kayah nodded as she unlocked the front door.

$$\infty\infty\infty$$

Kayah wandered the house, waiting to see if Bear would even show. She was standing in the doorway of her parent's bedroom when Onyx approached her and rested his chin on her shoulder.

"You know they say that when wolves die, our souls return to Aadya. So if we did good things, we would end up in paradise in Elysian Fields."

"So what happens to us if we are rotten and evil?"

"We will end up in the fiery depths of Tartarus."

"Well, that doesn't sound very promising."

"Why?"

"Because baby sister, I am a monster. I have killed people and wolves. I have to drink blood to survive."

"Let me cure you. Please, Onyx," Kayah pleaded.

"No. The bloodlust is too strong. I am afraid I couldn't stop, and I would kill you even if I did let you. I still need blood to survive."

"Onyx, you have looked after me almost all my life. I trust you. I know you would never hurt me. Our sibling bond is too strong for that to happen. If you let me cure you, you can have an everyday life. You would be mortal again; you could have kids, a house, a mortgage, and do whatever you wanted."

"We can talk about this later. We have more important things that must be handled right now."

"Besides the obvious. What else is there?" she asked.

"Like, what do you want to do with the house?"

"I don't know. Of course, I want to get rid of it because of the bad memories, but when I think about it, the good ones outweigh the bad ones. What do you suggest we do with it?"

"Kayah, the house was left to you. You can do what you want with it. But, I suggest keeping the place for us to stay when we have events up here. That way, we are safe and don't have to stay at the clubhouse."

"I like that idea. But we need to gut it out and make it our own."

"Come on, let's go find your man and my girl. See if they have heard anything."

Kayah nodded and looked at her parent's room one last time be for shutting the door to the room and dwelling on the past. Dezra and Demon were sitting in the living room, Dezra on the couch and Demon sitting in her dad's favorite chair. She walked over and plopped down in Demon's lap and leaned against him.

"Have you talked to Bear?"

"Yes, he said he is just outside of town. He said he would stop and pick up some beer and be right here."

"I don't like it...it doesn't smell right," Dezra said, wrinkling her nose.

It wasn't long before they heard Bear's truck pull down the driveway. Demon's body started to shake with anger. To help him calm down, Kayah placed a kiss on his pulse point under his jaw. She felt some tension leave her body, knowing it was working when his heart rate slowed. When Bear knocked on the door, Kayah opened the door and let him in. Bear sat the paper bag on the coffee table, and Kayah pushed the door, making it shut and the lock slide in place. Then she went back to her spot on Demon's lap.

"Hey guys, I want to say I am sorry once again for missing your wedding."

"You missed one hell of a party," Dezra said, snuggling into Onyx's side.

"So you two are an item now?" asked Bear.

"Yea, what of it!" Onyx growled, wrapping an arm around her and pulling her closer.

"Nothing, man. I am happy for you. I am just wondering how it's possible."

"Because my brother is a part of this pack and may choose any mate he wants."

"Well, to be technical, I hit on him first," Dezra said, showing Onyx a genuine smile.

"That is awesome. Welcome, man; I am glad Kayah has family again," Bear stammered.

Kayah could tell he had messed up because his heart rate started rising. Bear quickly changed the subject; he reached into the bag and pulled out a six-pack of beer.

He handed Demon and Kayah a beer and asked, "So you decided to sell the place?"

"Yeah, the memories from that night are just too much," Kayah said, taking the beer.

"Memories? I always thought you were somewhere else the night they died."

"Nope, I was here. I saw the whole thing. First, I saw how they tortured my mother by cutting her all over her body; then, I watched all three of them as they rapped her and shot her in the head. All while making my father watch. Then I watched as my father wept over my mother. Finally, they executed him with one bullet to the side of his head. But do you know the silver lining in the shit show I was forced to watch?" she asked him.

As he took a drink, she noticed his hand shaking, and he shook his head, "No, what is it?"

"I know who they are, every one of them. But, fortunately, their days are numbered; there is only one more thing I need to work out before I kill them," she said calmly as she twisted the cap off her beer.

"Yea, what is that?" he said after clearing his throat.

"Do I let you leave here so you can run to Daddy and let him know I'm coming, Or do I let Demon rip your head off here and send him your head in a box?" Kayah asked, taking a drink.

"What...what are you talking about. Kayah, you are scaring me a little," Bear asked.

"I know you are a gray wolf. I also know you are the son of the Alpha. Your father executed my parents. All because my father told your daddy no. I was promised to Demon after I was born. But your dad wanted me to be mated with you. When my father said no, he killed my parents and sent you to spy on me as I grew up. You are older than me. You were born the same year as Onyx. I also know that when Onyx showed signs of the ancient bloodline, your dad had my brother taken by a creature created by a witch your pack is loyal to. That way, when my parents had another child, it would most likely be a female Omega. As I said, Bear, I know everything," she said, standing.

"You were meant to be mine; I was born before Demon. So it's not too late. I can still make you mine," Bear growled.

"Now you are delusional. It is too late; the par bond has been completed," Kayah laughed.

"The par bond is still new. If your mate dies, another can be bonded to you," Bear spat.

"How is Demon going to die?"

"Me. I will kill Demon and take you as mine."

"I beat your ass when we were in high school. Do you think you can take me now?" asked Demon.

Bear growled and shifted and lunged at Demon. Kayah waited until the right moment, lifted her foot, and connected with his chest, knocking him back. Dezra started getting off the couch to help her friends when Onyx gripped her arm and shook his head no.

"This is for the Alphas to take care of. They won't kill him here. His life must be taken before the pack for his sentence to be carried out."

Dezra nodded and sat back. When Bear hit the wall, he lost control of his form and faded back to his human form.

"Brother, will you please restrain that piece of shit so we can take him back to the clubhouse?" Demon asked.

"Yes, Alpha, at once."

Chapter 26

Back at the clubhouse, Kayah was satisfied with shutting the bar door and locking Bear in the cell under the building.

"Don't get comfortable; your hours are numbered," said Kayah as she turned to talk to Sid.

"Why did you bring him here?" asked Sid.

"Because he is being charged with treason. By pack law, his sentence will be carried out before the pack. We have enough betrayals in this pack to last a lifetime. Demon and I refuse to start our reign by breaking pack law to feed our need for justice."

"I understand. That was a good call. Your father would be proud. What do you need me to do?" asked Sid.

"I need a couple of wolves to guard his cell. I also want some wolves to standpoint and some for lookout. We don't know if he told any of The Hunters what he was doing," Kayah commanded.

"I will make it happen," said Sid walking away and pulling out his phone.

Shortly, two wolves loyal to Colby descended the stairs and approached her.

"You can finish preparations for tonight. Hogan and I will be keeping guard."

"What is your name?"

"Seth," he answered.

"It is nice to meet you. However, no one enters, no one talks to him, and no one lays a finger on him. Is that clear?"

"Yes, Alpha."

"I will ensure someone brings food down for you and the traitor," said Kayah.

"Thank you, Alpha."

Kayah nodded and jogged up the stairs. After she shut the door, she leaned against it and closed her eyes to gather her thoughts. *Fuck I know he is a traitor, but he was also a friend. There is no way he was faking the friendship his whole life. Was he forced by his father to do this? All the answers will come out tonight.*

∞∞∞

An hour before the meeting, Kayah found Demon sitting in a chair, leaning against the wall. His head was tipped back, and his eyes were closed. Kayah walked up to him and pushed on his knee, making the chair sit correctly.

"Babe, why did you do that?"

"Didn't your mother ever teach you that all four chair legs are meant to touch the floor?" she smirked.

"Does it look like my mamma is here? No, I didn't think so."

"Oooh. Aren't you in a pissy mood?"

"Ya, think!" Demon snapped.

"Well, excuse me. I will leave you to your pissiness and find Dezra," she snapped back.

Demon let her get two steps away before he snatched her by the back of her jeans and pulled her onto his lap.

"Listen, Wife..."

"Excuse me?" she asked, raising her eyebrow.

"I just wanted to say I'm sorry. I don't mean to take it out on you," he said as he rested his forehead on hers.

"I know a lot is going on. Plus, the meeting tonight, and then we have The Hunters to deal with."

"I am not worried about that fucker. He will meet his end tonight. I am not concerned about the Hunters. Their days are numbered. I am worried about my dad. I just called the hospital and talked to Mom."

"What did they say?"

"He still hasn't woken up yet. The doc says that he still has internal bleeding. Baby, I don't know what I will do if he dies. This is just my dad; you lost your mom and dad. I don't know how you survived all these years without them."

Kayah pulled back and cupped his face in her hands. She

watched as tears trickled down his cheeks and thought. *How can this Alpha that dominated me two nights ago fall to pieces in my hands?*

"Because I had you. Demon, you have been my strength my whole life. So let me be yours now," she said, kissing him softly.

Demon wrapped his arms around Kayah and buried his face in her chest; when she rested her head on his and wrapped her arms around him, he finally let go. When his body stopped shaking from silent weeping, he looked up at his mate with tear-stained cheeks.

"Thank you, my love; I feel a lot better."

"I got you, baby, now and forever."

Demon kissed Kayah and stood holding her in his arms. "Our parents were right; we were meant for each other."

"Well, I am glad you think so because you are kinda stuck with me now," Kayah huffed.

Demon laughed as he set her feet on the ground, "I love you. I need to finish pulling myself together before we start the meeting." Then he kissed her and walked off, leaving her temper on a low simmer.

∞∞∞

Kayah and Demon stood before their pack and studied the mixture of wolves and humans gathered in one room. Then she looked over at Demon and nodded.

Demon: *"I hear by call this meeting to order. We have three things of business to take care of tonight. We have a new wolf joining the pack, new members and races joining the pack, and a sentence to be carried out. Is everyone in agreement?"*

All: *"Yes, Alpha."*

Demon: *"First order of business. Onyx, come and join us."*

Onyx stood, slowly climbed the stairs, and stood before Demon and Kayah.

Demon: *"I am going to ask you a question. By wolf law, you must answer honestly. Do you wish to join this pack or live out your days as a lone wolf?"*

Onyx: *"Alpha, I choose the pack. I have lived my whole life as a lone wolf."*

Demon: *"If you join this pack, you will be bound to uphold and live by pack law. Do you agree?"*

Onyx: *"Yes, Alpha."*

Demon: *"If you agree, drop to your knees to show your submission to your Alphas."*

Onyx knelt and then went to all fours while bowing his head.

Kayah: *"You must now recite the pack oath."*

Onyx: *"I hereby submit and obey my Alphas and only my Alphas. I will help my Alphas by upholding pack law. If any of these laws are broken, I hereby acknowledge my punishment could result in banishment or even death. If I witness any wolf breaking pack law and fail to report it to my Alphas, I will have the same fate as the guilty party. I renounce my lone wolf status and acknowledge this pack as my own."*

Kayah: *"Stand and obey your Alphas."*

Onyx's heart raced as he stood and looked at Kayah and Demon, waiting for the final words.

Kayah: *"Onyx, you are now part of this pack. Welcome home."*

Kayah watched as tears started to swim through Onyx's eyes. He blinked, holding them back. Finally, Demon held out his hand for Onyx to take.

"Welcome home, brother."

When he looked back at Kayah, he had no time to react. She grabbed hold of him and pulled him into a hug. "Welcome home, big brother."

Before Onyx could return to his seat, Kayah spoke again.

Kayah: *"Onyx"*

Onyx: *"Yes, Alpha."*

Kayah: *"You just took an oath to obey. Correct?"*

Onyx: *"Yes, Alpha."*

Kayah: *"Turn and face me."*

When Onyx turned, he knew what she was about to say. He started to back away, shaking his head.

Kayah: *"Onyx, stop!"*

Demon leaned over and whispered, "Kayah, this is an abuse of power. You can not do this."

"Back off, Demon, and trust me."

Kayah*: "Onyx, I stand before you not as your Alpha but as your sister. I stand before our pack and beg you to let me help you. I stand before our pack to announce that I trust you. Please let me cure you."*

Onyx looked over at Dezra and motioned her to join him. When she was by his side, he upholstered his Glock and handed it to Dezra. Then he looked at Demon, "If I can't control myself, pull me off her, then Dezra is to shoot me in the heart." Next, he looked at Dezra, "I know I haven't told you, but I love you. You are my whole world. But I need you to shoot me if I become a danger to Kayah."

"I am not worried; you will be able to. I believe in you," Dezra said as she kissed him.

Onyx approached Kayah and asked, "Are you sure about this?"

"One hundred percent."

Onyx took a deep breath and showed the wolves that were now his family, the monster he hid from everyone. He cupped the back of Kayah's neck and tipped her head enough to show her skin move with every beat of her heart. Then, he bared his fangs and sank them into Kayah's neck, causing her to scream and go quiet. As he fed, he pictured his sister's smiling face. With Kayah in the forefront of his brain, the bloodlust was gone. When he started to feel the change take over, he released Kayah to find her alive and smiling at him.

Onyx fell to his knees and held his rolling stomach; Dezra quickly dropped to her knees, yelling, "Get a garbage can."

They got the garbage can just as he started throwing up. The fresh blood he had just drunk came up first, then black blood the color of oil. When he was done, it left him shaking and a body covered in sweat. The first thing that came out of his mouth was, "Dezra, will you be my mate for life?"

Dezra looked at Kayah and asked, "Did this cracker just ask

me what I think he did?"

Onyx fought to reach his feet and looked at her again, "Yes, my chocolate bunny! Will you be my mate for life?"

"Yes, White Boy. I will be your mate."

Onyx smiled at Kayah, saying, "Thank you for believing in me."

"Any time, brother."

Onyx took Dezra's hand and started walking back to their seats when he stumbled, and Demon caught him by the arm, "Hey, you okay?"

"No, I am weak. I need to feed."

Before anyone could say anything, Dezra took out her knife and cut her arm, shoving it in Onyx's mouth and forcing him to drink, "Well, if I am going to be his wife, I guess I better start taking care of my man now."

This caused the entire room to chuckle.

"Now, if you excuse us, I will take my man, and you all can finish the meeting."

Kayah and Demon took the next hour to swear the humans into the pack. However, she saved her uncle for last.

Kayah: *John, do you agree to live by pack law, protect our secret, and love us as you would your own family?"*

John: *"Yes, with this responsibility, I will only see them as my family. I may only be human, but I will live by wolf pack law and recognize you as my Alphas. I also acknowledge if I break these laws, the punishment could be banishment or even death. I will also be held responsible if I know that pack laws are being broken and that I will see the same fate as the guilty."*

Kayah: *"From this day forward, I acknowledge you as a pack member. Welcome home."*

John: *"Thank you, Alpha."*

As John returned to his seat, Demon looked at Sid and nodded. Then, he and Onyx headed downstairs to collect Bear.

Kayah: *"Now we have some unpleasant business to take care of. For everyone that just joined the pack, let this be a lesson. This wolf is being charged with treason. For years he has lived with the*

Dire Wolf pack of New Orleans. He attended pack meeting and was even raised by this pack. He was sent to deceive the pack when I was adopted by the Alpha of the Dire Wolves, Colby, who now lies in the hospital fighting for his life. As you all know, my parents were killed by The Hunters, the Gray Wolves. The Alpha of the Gray Wolves is his father. He has reported back to his father, telling our secrets that resulted in Dezra and myself being kidnapped and hospitalized. We believe he is also responsible for what happened to Colby. On the night Colby was jumped, Bear was missing. Since his crime is against me and the Dire Wolves, his judgment and sentence will be deemed by Demon."

Demon: *"As Alpha and mate to Kayah, I sentence this wolf to death for treason. Does everyone agree with this judgment?"*

All: *"Yes, Alpha."*

Kayah: *"Do you have anything to say?"*

Bear: *"You were meant to be mine. I regret nothing. I was the one that put Colby in a coma. My plan would have worked if Colby had never told you about your past and who you are. Demon would* *have been mated with someone else, and I would have been mated*

with you. It looks like the Gray Wolves took both of your daddies,"

Bear laughed.

Demon: *"I have had enough of your bullshit to last a lifetime."*

Demon let his anger take control of his wolf form and let the Primal Alpha loose. But, instead of shifting into his standard wolf form, he transformed into a werewolf standing on his hind legs. With each step he took, the wood on the stage creaked and groaned under his weight.

"What the fuck are you?" Bear yelled as he pissed on himself and dropped to his knees.

"He is one of the Alphas you betrayed," Sid said as he pick Bear up making him stand.

Demon slashed Bear's chest, turning it to ribbons. Kayah could see his heart beating behind his ribcage. Before Bear could pass out from the loss of blood Demon reached in Bear's chest breaking the ribs and pulled his beating heart out. The last thing Bear saw was his own heart stop beating. Demon's form faded while he was still holding Bear's heart and said, "Put it in a box and give it to his father. Oh make sure you gift wrap it, make sure you sign the card Love Kayah and Demon. Then Demon dropped the heart and said, "This meeting is now closed. Sid would you please have some wolves help you clean this up?"

"Yes, Alpha. What would you like us to do with the body?" Sid asked.

"I know we normally burn the bodies of the fallen, but he doesn't deserve it. Actually pack it in ice, I will deliver the body to his father myself. Make sure that heart makes it to The Hunters. They will make sure it goes to their Alpha."

Chapter 27

After Demon was done giving his orders, he walked off and disappeared. Kayah found him in the shower, standing under the hot water with his forehead on the wall. Saying nothing, she undressed and stepped in behind him. Kayah laid her cheek on his back and wrapped her arms around him, letting the water wash over them. She knew he wasn't ready to talk when he covered her arms with his. When he finally let go, she stepped back. Demon turned, squirted some shampoo in his hand, and started washing her hair.

"Demon, what are you doing?"

"What does it look like I'm doing? I am washing your hair," Demon said with a slight smile.

"Well, if you are going to wash my hair, I get to wash your body," she said, grabbing the body wash.

Kayah squeezed a quarter-size dollop of body wash into her hands, rubbed it on Demon's chest, and slowly covered his body in suds. The mood quickly changed from caring caresses to needy. Demon turned off the water, grabbed a towel off the rack, and wrapped it around Kayah. Next, he snagged another towel and wrapped it around his hips; with a devilish grin, he picked up Kayah, carried her like a sack of potatoes into the bedroom, and tossed her on the bed.

Demon crawled onto the bed beside her, kissing her shoulder and moving slowly to her neck. Before he could blink, Kayah had him pinned, and the roles were reversed. She straddled him with his arms pinned under her knees. She bent down and whispered, "Remember, I am an Alpha too. I don't mind submitting to you sometimes; sometimes, you will honor me by doing the same. Now be a good boy, and don't move until you are told."

When Kayah smiled, Demon saw that she had excellent control over shifting body parts. She had stayed in human form but extended her canines. Kayah sank her teeth into his left peck above his heart; her bite was deep enough that it would scar. Demon pulled his arms free and griped the outsides of her thighs hard enough to leave prints. Before she crushed her mouth to his, she said, "I thought I told you not to move." Demon could tell from the kiss that Kayah retracted her canines. She moved slowly, nipping and kissing down his body, taking him to the edge of losing control. Demon stayed true to his Alpha and didn't move. Using her strength, Kayah pulled the towel out from underneath Demon; with a wicked smile, she tore the towel into strips and bound his hands. When Kayah had him where she wanted him, she continued her assault. When she placed her hands on his hips to hold him still, she watched his eyes close when she took him into her mouth. By the time he came, he was begging Kayah to release him.

"Not yet." was all she said before she straddled him.

She moved her hips into the correct position and slowly took him. Kayah watched the reactions she caused with every move she made. Finally, when she came, and the Alpha in her was sated, she collapsed onto his chest. Demon moved his arms above his head and placed his bound hand on her back.

"Baby, whenever you want to be in charge, go right ahead. You will get no complaints from me. There is just one thing."

"Yeah, what is that?" she asked sleepily.

"Can you untie me now?" he asked.

"Yes," she giggled. "Let me up."

Kayah worked on the knots to unbind her handsome man when he said, "I love you, Kayah."

"I love you too."

"I would love to go for round two, but you are tired, and I have a new wound to dress."

Kayah lay in the bed next to him on her side. "I was just showing you I am just as much an Alpha in the bedroom as you."

"Baby, I never doubted you one bit."

∞∞∞

After Demon and Kayah checked to ensure the clubhouse was locked and secure, they headed to their room. Not long after they had fallen asleep; Sid started banging on their door.

"Kayah, Demon…wake up!"

Demon hopped out of bed and answered the door to pure chaos. "What the hell is going on?"

"They're here!" answered Sid.

When Demon looked back at Kayah, she was dressed and slipping her father's gun holster over her shoulders.

"The Alpha is mine," she said, pushing past Demon.

Demon quickly dressed and ran, searching for Kayah.

Kayah was in the meeting room, barking orders and telling people where to go.

"Dezra and Onyx, I want you to stay close to Demon and me. Seth, please find some people and take the left side. Adam, do the same on the right. Remember, everyone, humans only have our strength. They are still very breakable and don't have our healing abilities. Onyx, do we know how many are here?"

"It looks like a couple of messengers; that's it."

"Doesn't smell right...I don't like it," commented Dezra.

"I don't know what you are smelling, but I get that feeling, too," Kayah agreed.

"Shilo, let in... let in the messengers, but watch your six."

"Yes, Alpha," he said before jogging off.

"Where are all the old ladies?" Kayah asked.

"They are safe downstairs," Dezra answered.

Kayah heard the footsteps as they approached; when the door opened, her anger spiked. One of the men that were responsible just walked into her clubhouse.

"We have come to give you a message."

"What would that be?"

"Whoever killed the Alpha's son must turn themselves over by noon, or you all die."

"I have a message you can return to that spineless piece of

shit you call an Alpha," Kayah growled.

"Watch your mouth, bitch. Who do you think you are? A man needs to show you the only thing that a woman is good for."

"First of all, you come into my den and try and tell me what to do. That was your second mistake."

"Your den, huh? If that was my second mistake, what was my first," asked the man that killed her parents, smirking.

"Killing my parents."

"There's no proof that I killed anyone."

"I was there. I saw everything, and I know who all of you are. So this is my message. You tell that sorry excuse of an Alpha I am coming for him and his VP."

"There is no way you are Kayah?"

"I am Kayah. I am the Alpha of this pack. And I know you are one of the men that killed my parents. I saw everything."

"We searched that house. You were nowhere to be found," he spat.

"I was there. I saw how you tied my father to a chair, tortured my mother then the three of you raped her. Then you executed them because they wouldn't tell you where I was at."

The smirk on his face fell; he knew she was telling the truth. "So what makes you think I will tell my Alpha anything?"

"Because you are the message," Kayah said as she pulled out her father's Glock and shot him between the eyes. "Now, get out of here and deliver my message. Take that piece of shit with you before he starts stinking up my den."

The Gray Wolves worked quickly, picking up their dead and leaving the clubhouse. Shilo watched as they loaded him into their truck and sped away. When the door was locked, Shilo joined Demon and Kayah and said, "Kayah, please remind me never to piss you off."

"She-Bitch are you okay?"

"Yes, why?" asked Kayah.

"Because you just blew someone away. I know he had it coming. But I mean, you just pulled out that Glock and Blam.

You blew that mother fucker away."

"Yes, I did. That makes two down and two to go."

Chapter 28

Demon watched Kayah as he stood at what he would call the war table, pointing at a map. He thought she looked badass, from the black tee shirt to the motorcycle boots. To top off the whole look, she was still wearing the gun she used to kill someone two hours ago. His mate was about to lead their pack into war. She must have felt him watching because when she looked up from the map, she locked eyes with Demon. He loved her with every fiber of his being. He loved how soft and pliable she was when she gave up control and submitted, and he loved the hard-as-steel Alpha she was.

He pushed off the wall and joined her at the head of the table, "What's the plan?"

"Sid and Onyx think we should let them bring the fight to us; Dezra and Shilo said we should take it to them."

"What do you want to do, Kayah?" asked Demon.

"I think we need to let them come to us. Only because we know our footing here, if we go to them, we will walk in blind."

"I agree. Let them come to us. They had no problem sending messengers this morning. Plus, they said they were coming here to kill us if I didn't show up by noon." Demon added.

"Then that's what we will do," Kayah said.

"Kayah, there is one more thing that you and Demon need to do," added Sid.

"What?" they asked.

"You two need to appoint someone on as your right hand. This person must be someone you trust with your life. Someone that will always have your back no matter what. I can not be this person."

"Why can't you?"

"Because I am Colby's. You each need to choose a person."

Demon looked at Shilo and remembered how he had always had his back, even when it came to Kayah.

"I choose Shilo," said Demon.

Shilo looked up from the notes he was taking and said, "Huh?"

"I have chosen you to be my right-hand man."

"Oh...Thank you. I am honored. I won't let you down. There is just one thing."

"What's that?"

"I will help you with anything in this world or the next, except be your right hand to do the do if you do something to piss her off and she withholds sex. You are taking care of yourself; I'm juss sayin.

Demon shook his head as everyone chucked, and Kayah smiled. "I am seriously rethinking my choice."

Shilo made everyone laugh harder when he held his hands up and shrugged his shoulders.

Kayah knew she was next to make a choice, and she looked at Dezra and then her brother. I am sorry, Onyx, I choose Dezra. She has been there for me through everything. She has been my ride-or-die since we were kids. There is no one I trust more than her.

Dezra looked at Kayah dumbfounded, "I thought you would pick your brother."

"No. We made a pact when we were children, 'Ride or Die, but never alone!' I love you."

"I love you too She-Bitch."

The rest of the day was quiet on all fronts. Kayah was kicked back onto one of the couches, watching her wolves in their different groups. Some were playing cards, some were watching t.v., and some were resting. She watched Demon and Shilo as they laughed and talked.

The war between the packs started when the sky turned to night.

When Kayah and Demon stepped outside, there was a pack of Gray Wolves, and in the front stood their Alpha and his VP.

"Where is my son BITCH!" the Alpha snarled.

"In hell. Don't worry. You will be joining him soon enough." Kayah growled back.

"I see you received our gift and my mate's message." taunted Demon.

"How do I know that it is my son's heart?"

"Bring the traitor's body," yelled Demon.

Onyx and Shilo carried out Bear's body and dropped it before the Alpha. The Alpha screamed and dropped to his knees, "What did he do to deserve this?" he asked, looking at Kayah and Demon.

"He was tried and sentenced by pack law; Bear was found guilty of treason. He was sentenced to death."

"How was he charged with treason when the Alpha of this pack is fighting for his life, if he is not already dead?"

"I guess he didn't tell you everything. When Demon and I were married, we became the Alphas of this pack," answered Kayah.

"Who are you? You are nothing but a Bitch in a pack."

Kayah's body vibrated with anger, and she was fighting her instinct to shift. Demon could tell she was having trouble staying focused. He leaned over and talked to where she was the only one that could hear him. "Hold on, baby, just a little longer. Then you can shift and rip them to shreds.

"Who am I? I am Kayah. I am the one you seek."

"Kayah," he smirked as he stood. "So we finally meet. Why don't we stop all this foolishness and come with me now? If you go with me and carry my pack's pups, I will let your precious wolves live."

"No. But I will tell you what is going to happen. You are going to pay for your sins today. You will die for what you did to my parents and my brother. I will have justice for my family," Kayah said calmly.

The tone of Kayah's voice made the pack, and the VP take a couple of steps back.

"You are already putting a stain on your father's name. Your father was against wolves using guns. But yet I see you are wearing his. When your father would fight, he would fight in his proper form. I guess the legends were wrong. You are just a regular wolf; that must be weak because you and your pack are hiding behind guns."

"Now is the time, Kayah," Demon said calmly.

"Guns? Who said I was going to use guns," Kayah said, letting the holster hit the ground.

Like her mate, she let the anger take control of the shift. In Kayah's werewolf form, she stood over six foot seven, her coat was pure white, and her eyes were electric blue. When she stood on her hind legs, Demon smiled.

"My mate doesn't need a gun. If I were you, I would start saying your prayers."

The Alpha of the Gray Wolves took a step back to assess the situation.

"Look, maybe we can work this out. I will give you the ones responsible for your parent's death. We can work out some kind of alliance."

"That would be a hard no from both the Alphas of this pack," Demon answered.

Kayah tipped her head back and howled, letting her pack know it was time to drop the weapons and shift.

"See, one of the beautiful things that were kept out of the stories was that every wolf that attended our wedding gained some of Kayah's abilities," once again Demon taunted.

"Well, that doesn't say much for her mate. Unfortunately, it looks like you got the short end of the stick," The Alpha spat back.

Demon looked up at his mate and touched her soft fur; when he looked back at the Alpha, his eyes glowed, "Me, she gave me the best gift aside from being my mate. She gave me all of her abilities," Demon said as he let loose the Primal Alpha, he held inside.

Kayah and Demon looked like a complete Yin Yang, with her pure white fur and his black as night. Kayah and Demon tipped their heads back and howled again, letting their wolves loose.

While the moon was at its apex, Kayah fought with her mate and pack. The humans fought alongside the wolves for the first time in history. Kayah fought wolves as she crossed the parking lot, working her way to the only human in the Gray Wolves' pack. The man with his hair pulled back in a low tail. The man she remembers as the first to rape her mother. Three wolves jumped when she stood before him, sinking their teeth into her sides and shoulder and making Kayah land on all fours.

John saw the wolves attack Kayah and yelled, "Hold on, baby girl, I am on my way."

John picked up Nyko's Glock and started shooting the Gray wolves as he made his way to Kayah. When his head was turned, a wolf sank their teeth into his left arm, shredding it and rendering it useless. Using the Glock in his right hand, he placed the barrel on the wolf's forehead and pulled the trigger, splattering John's face in blood. Kayah looked his way when he screamed, and three more shots were fired. Kayah watched in horror as the Alpha of the Gray Wolves ripped her uncle's throat out.

Kayah howled and found her strength; Dezra came out of nowhere like a streak of white lightning. She gripped the wolf on Kayah's right hip and pulled. Dezra fought to pin the gray wolf, and when there was an opening, she sank her teeth into its neck and twisted, snapping it. Then, as Kayah freed herself from the wolf on her shoulder, Dezra worked on the one on her left hip; instead of breaking its neck, she ripped its throat out. Finally, when Kayah held the wolf, she gripped one of its front legs and head and pulled. It made a sickening pop with the head ripped from its body. When Kayah looked at Dezra, she noticed her beautiful white fur was matted and dripping with blood.

Kayah searched for her prey; she opened her senses and listened for a different heartbeat rhythm. Kayah's left ear twitched, and she followed the sound. She and Dezra found the VP hiding in a truck bed, quivering. Kayah looked down at Dezra and nodded, letting her know this was her kill. Dezra leaped into the truck bed and bared her teeth. She remembered the horror story Kayah had told her. How this man found pleasure in drawing a knife across her mother's naked body, how this man reveled in being the first one to rape Kayah's mother. Dezra took her claws and slowly turned his chest into ribbons, then Dezra worked on the legs shredding clothing and flesh. Finally, when he begged her to stop, Dezra granted him death by sinking her teeth into his crotch and ripping off his manhood.

Kayah dragged him behind her as he bled to death and dropped him before the Gray Wolf Alpha. The Alpha's form faded to human, and he fell to his knees.

"Kayah, you have won, can't you see that? Let me take what is left of my wolves and leave. You have taken my son and my best friend. Can this be over? I am sorry for what I did; I paid for my sins with my son's death."

Dezra shifted and said, "Hold him."